Tina Maurine

Vexed

A Uniform & Lace Romance Novella

Noah's Story in St. John, BVI
~Novella between Volition & Veneration~

Tina Maurine

This book is a work of fiction. Names, characters, places and incidents are products of the author's imagination and are not to be construed as real. Any resemblance to actual events, locales, organizations, or persons living or dead, is entirely coincidental.

COPYRIGHT

Trient Press

3375 S Rainbow Blvd

#81710, SMB 13135

Las Vegas,NV 89180

Ordering Information:

Quantity sales. Special discounts are available on quantity purchases by corporations, associations, and others. For details, contact the publisher at the address above.

Orders by U.S. trade bookstores and wholesalers. Please contact Trient Press: Tel: (775) 996-3844; or visit www.trientpress.com.

Printed in the United States of America

Publisher's Cataloging-in-Publication data
Maurine, Tina

A title of a book :Vexed

ISBN Hard Cover:978-1-953975-87-4
Paperback: 978-1-953975-15-7
E-book: 978-1-953975-88-1

Tina Maurine

Dedication

To my sweet B., T. & K.

The world we've created together is perfect—
and this, my third book, is just the icing on the top.
Thanks for your neverending support and love.

To My Crew

Without you, I'd never have gotten this far.
Thanks for believing in my abilities, supporting my dream, and
making my work shine.
Truly, THANK YOU.

Tina Maurine

Vexed

-PROLOGUE-

Unscrupulous piece of shit! Dane was a dodgy fucker, and there was no doubt in my mind what that ass-hat wanted from my girl… *or whatever the fuck Tessa currently is.*

We left the remaining drunks and misfits who still lingered at Dane's party and swaggered towards base. Thankfully, when we reached the gate, I didn't recognize the unfortunate security-fucker who had been standing gate duty since 2230 last night. *That's all I need; rumors about how drunk I am getting back to my command.*

We all pulled out our IDs silently, and he waved us through.

Right, Left. Right, Left. Right, Left. I'd reduced my thoughts to just putting one foot in front of the other as I marched towards my barracks, but slowly, my thoughts drifted to the way I'd behaved around Tessa. To Tessa. I shook my head and shielded my eyes from the blaringly bright sun, made only brighter by the countless shots I'd consumed at that Icelandic rat's pad. *What did Tessa ever see in Dane?*

As nonsensical as it was—her liking Dane—it gave me no right to confront her at the party by having her compare her relationship with me to the relationship she'd once had with him. Shit, then to step up on him like that as we were leaving… I shook my head. *Shit, I'd acted like an ass. Even though they had passionate, MIND-BLOWING sex two months before she met me.*

I ran my fingers through my hair, cursing silently at the greatest fuck up of the night. *My timing for telling her I was planning to get back with Vi couldn't have been any worse. I hurt her because I was jealous of HIM.*

Marching on, I felt like I was swirling in a mid-conscious state, part silent movie and part amusement park fun house.

"What was that, Ari?"

My eyes snapped up from the reflective pavement that had mesmerized me. *Her voice…* Tessa. *My Tessa, and I'm blowing it.*

Ari aimed one of his million-dollar smiles directly at Tessa. "Baby girl, you told Dane you'd keep that in mind. Keep what?" He swayed back and forth. "Is he throwing another party? Did you get another invite?"

Tessa grinned, "Yeah, something like that," she replied, but she didn't offer any further explanation.

She didn't have to. "He wanted a piece of ass, dumb shit," I snarled under my breath and couldn't disguise the snort that followed. I saw Tessa cock her head back in my direction, and then, with a shrug, she shook her head in what I could only imagine was disgust—*FUCK!*

If my mood weren't so royally fucked, it really would've been a gorgeous morning. The wind wasn't blowing, so the cold wasn't unbearable for a change. We trudged on— *Right, left. Right, left. Right, left. Right, left*—maybe ten minutes. It brought us about a quarter of the way back to our respective barracks, but, Jeezus, I just couldn't get the way I'd treated Tessa at the party or after out of my mind. To make matters worse, my head was already pounding with a brutal headache—stage one of the hangover that was sure to follow.

Fuck it, it's now or never. I mustered up the courage— real courage not the shit I'd derived from the bottle last night— and made my way up to the front of the pack where Tessa was. I shouldered up next to her, "Hey, Beautiful." I didn't really know where to start, but my shame over the way I'd behaved showed in my face… I'd never been able to hide my feelings from her.

"Hey," she said, completely deadpan and obviously still angry with me… as I expected she would be.

"You know, I'm… I'm sorry. It's just that…"

She put her hand up to stop me. We both glanced over our shoulders and took inventory of everyone. Dirk and Ari had grouped together in the back, bullshitting and razzing Sammie and Kari about something. Sammie and Kari looked like a scene out of Night of the Living Dead. *Shit, they look even rougher than I do!* It was hard not to chuckle.

"You know, Noah," Tessa whispered, "I just don't know what to make of you. Today, you're acting all jealous over a guy I slept with months before I met you. On the same day, you alluded to WHEN you get back with Vi." She shrugged. "I mean, how am I supposed to take that?" Tessa's voice cracked, and she hugged herself.

"I know," I muttered, hanging my head. "I don't know why I care about Dane either." I looked up, searching for her eyes, and when mine met hers, the energy I felt jolted me with a shudder. "Tess, just the thought of his greasy hands on you, and him and you… FUCK!" I wrestled as the onslaught of wave after wave of confusion hit me—frustration, anger, jealousy—and I scrubbed my hands over my face to ease the tension, then through my too-long hair, before sucking in a deep breath. "Even though a piece of me is torn and wants to stay, you know I have to go." I sighed, unable to find less painful words to state that I still hadn't changed my plans.

Why are you doing this to yourself, to her? I thought irately, watching as she angrily wiped a tear off her liquor-reddened cheek. *You've been searching years for a woman— any woman—who could live up to, let alone replace, the memory of our night together at her enlistment party years ago. Do something before you lose the woman that, in spite of everything, you still hunger for!*

A hazy image of my unknown daughter fluttered across my consciousness, hardening my resolve yet again. *Your happiness is not as important as Suri having a father. Be a man, Garren.*

I watched Tessa slip further away from me with each wounded tear she shed and swiped angrily at. We trudged forward across the wet pavement that reflected the sun invasively into our eyes. A million thoughts swirled in my head, but only one made perfect sense. I sighed heavily, "Beautiful." I stopped, taking Tessa's shoulders and turning her to face me. "You and I… there's just something I can't explain, and it unnerves me, upends me. Fuck, Tessa, look at what you do to me. I can't lose you no matter what happens." *There. I'd told her how much she means to me.*

"Well, you should've thought of that long before now…" she said remorsefully, hanging her head, her shoulders slack and lifeless.

Tessa's painful tone and the way her eyes refused to meet mine saddened me. *Didn't she hear what I said? I'm sorry for the way I acted, and I can't lose you. I said it plain as day…* My dark sapphire eyes remained focused on her, begging her to look up at me and when she did, what I saw there did anything but lift my spirits. I knew, before she even opened her luscious, so-kissable mouth, that she HAD, in fact, heard everything I'd said, and that it hadn't been enough.

"I just can't find it in me to play second-fiddle. I want to be with someone who wants me…"

"But I DO!"

"…and knows it, Noah. Someone who chooses me above anyone else." At this, she shook free of my hold on her and looked to Sammie, who had nearly caught up.

"Hey, Sam," she called out buoyantly, "wanna head to the Café Barista for a strong cup of joe?"

She looked from me to Tessa, to the guys, and jogged the few steps to catch up to us. "You bet I do!" Smiling, she wrapped her arm around Tessa's sagging shoulders. "Come on, hooka, let's ditch these losers," she looked pointedly at me, "and get the best damn cup of coffee you've ever had. You deserve it after last night." She hooked elbows with Tessa. Hands deep in their pockets for warmth, they headed off alone in the direction of the base coffee shop.

"Forgive me?" I called after her, my voice that of a stranger, unhinged and unbalanced.

Without even breaking stride, Tessa shook her head and shouted, "I *ALWAYS* fucking do!"

I fell into step with Dirk and Ari, as Kari ran to catch up with the other two girls for a strong cup of coffee. We walked in silence. We'd already walked close to halfway; a good twenty minutes remained before we reached Tessa's barracks… maybe ten before we reached mine, but that's not where we were headed. We trudged on, noticing duty vans and buses taking personnel to their hangars, and I'd never been as glad as I was now that I wasn't off to do the same. My head ached, but it was *nothing* compared to the surprising ache in my chest that was already threatening to break me. *What have I done?*

"I sure hope Vi's worth it." Ari startled me. It was as though he'd taken up residence in my thoughts and knew what I'd been thinking.

I looked directly at him, "Me too, brother, me too…"

"Well, if you aren't sure, Noah…"

I interrupted Dirk, "I am. It's just really hard, ya know? I mean, Tessa's the girl who ended my search and put my soul at rest after losing Pallavi. Granted, it was only at rest for that night, at her party…" I pulled at my hair in frustration and ran my hands over my face—*what I must look like right now!*

"Well, you're not gone yet." Dirk's voice pulled me from my self-pity. "You have time to say goodbye—in a way that isn't a final goodbye." He nudged me, "Maybe all you two need is a little time to gain a different perspective about this time apart."

"All I know," Ari chimed in, "is that Tess is really looking forward to our detachment to Turkey while you're gone."

Dirk and I both looked at him, and in unison, we ordered, "Shut Up!" Then we all laughed, joking the last few blocks to the barracks.

We fumbled with the girls' doorknob. It was AFU, and all I had to do was jiggle it a bunch until the lock popped. We let ourselves in, and Dirk and I grabbed beer out of Tessa and Sammie's mini-fridge, offering one to Ari.

"Here's to your trip, man." Ari held out his beer in a toast, "I hope you meet your beautiful daughter, have a reinvigorating leave while you're away from this hellhole, and find the answers you're looking for."

"Hear, hear!"

"I'll toast to that!" I tapped my bottle to theirs and the chink of the glass echoed in the empty room, resounding in my wounded heart.

It wasn't long before Dirk lay drunk and snoring on Sammie's bed, and Ari had taken up residence in the Blue Beast, their oversized chair.

"Hey," I said, motioning to the bed, then the door, "sleep's looking pretty good right now, and if Tess and I are gonna try to make things right… the Blue Beast might not be the best place to sleep off your hangover."

Ari chuckled and struggled to sit up, finally throwing his legs down to right his upper body. He stood unevenly, "Yeah, man," he yawned, "I guess you're right." He headed to the door, cracked it and looked back over at me. "Girls like Tessa are one in a million," he paused and swayed as he grabbed the door before slurring, "I've never met anyone like her." Ari swayed before steadying himself against the doorjamb, "But to have two! *Two* girls so amazing… I mean, this other girl must be a real prize if you're throwing Tess away for her."

I'm not throwing her away, asshole! I just… I just have to go see about Pallavi and Suri is all!

He mumbled something I couldn't make out, then he pointed at me. "Just know, buddy, if you fuck this up with Tess… I'll be here to pick up the pieces."

The fuck you will!

I heard him mutter something about '*as a friend,*' then he closed the door behind him.

I flicked off the light switch and dressed down to my boxer-briefs, climbing into Tessa's bed. Her smell enveloped me, making me uncomfortably hard while I drifted off in a fitful, half-drunken, half-hungover slumber.

I started awake to emerald green eyes peering into mine. Tessa's red locks grazed my chest, her tits pert and sexy as hell in only her camisole. I reached up and pulled her to me, hugging her tightly. "Should I go?"

I couldn't see the war waging within her, but felt her tense, then pull away, before she settled back into me. "No. I guess I'm kind of glad you're here," she whispered softly, careful not to awaken Dirk and Sammie.

I shifted again and groggily positioned her so she spooned against me. "Tessa?"

"Yes, Noah?"

"I leave in a few hours."

"I know."

"I just wanted to say goodbye to you one last time. I really hope you're okay with me being here. It's just, I needed…"

She leaned up on her elbow, smiling back at me, "Yeah. You know, I truly felt the need to say a final goodbye to you too, one that wasn't so… angry." She pulled my arms tightly around her waist and snuggled more closely into my body. My member instantly hardened, not nearly as tired as I was, and, damn it, Tessa ground her ass into me, causing a shudder to rake my body and pulse through my cock.

"Tessa…?" I asked, only slightly shocked at her actions.

"Mmm-hmm?" she said in a smooth purr.

"Let me make love to you. I think about you every night when I'm alone, and I pray that if I get some closure, you'll stop haunting me."

I hoped Tessa heard me, but now, this moment lay in her hands. Just having her near me elevated my soul, made everything else, no matter how important, fade away. She was my vice, my bad habit that I couldn't ever get enough of. Right now, she was my everything. I needed one last fix.

I heard Dirk mutter something in a sleepy voice, and Sammie responded with, "Me too."

Tessa and I stilled, only our heavy, passion-laden breaths noticeable in an otherwise quiet room.

"My head," he muttered. "Need air."

"Let's go for a walk then," she replied softly. I heard Sammie and Dirk rise from the bed.

Her keys jingled as their soft footsteps swished across the floor, and the door clicked quietly in the jamb.

That door clicking was my go-light. My rough hands gripped at Tess's hip bones, pulling her, crushing her into my hard desire. Tessa was no innocent, and she reciprocated with rolling grinds of her ass against my cock. My hands navigated the curves of her body, flitting across her abdomen, up her ribs to her full, heaving breasts.

"If you don't stop me, I'm going to make love to you." My lips grazed the sensitive side of her neck, just below her ear, as my need and desire for her poured from my lips. My hands continued their demanding exploration against her pert tits, gently rolling and pinching her already hard nipples. Her soft mewling and uneven breaths spurred me on. My hand slid south into her faint suggestion of panties where I slid my middle finger through her moist lips. A moan caught in my throat, and a bead of need moistened the tip of my pulsating dick.

I edged us precariously close to the precipice of no return, as I traced lazy circles around her most sensitive bud before entering her with two fingers. Her sharp intake of heated breath nearly undid me.

In one well-practiced maneuver, I had her lying underneath me, my rigid cock resting at her apex. My dark blue depths penetrated her green cat eyes as I ground my hard sex into the sweetness between her eager thighs.

"Oh my God, Tessa. You have no idea how badly I've wanted to have you underneath me, writhing for me… and I can fucking tell you this much," I growled in a husky, passion-laden voice, "this time I'm going to give you more than a goddamn feel."

My mouth met hers with fierce passion. My lips melded with hers, branding her. Claiming her. Our lips danced to our own perfect beat with a ferocity that had only been matched that morning in the tour bus. Her tongue teased and sparred with mine. Damn it if I couldn't get enough of my sweet, sweet Tessa.

Her delicate hands entangled in my hair and pulled me back down to her. I sought her neck, and with each teasing nip and bite, her nails clawed across my back. This beautiful, sweet siren lay writhing before me, pulling at my hips, grinding her desire into my hard-as-fuck cock… asking me to do things to her that her lips refused to relinquish.

"Noah…"

"Mmm hmm." I nuzzled into her neck, teasing her as she spoke.

"Noah," I heard her swallow hard before continuing, "I want you to take me… fucking take me the way I want to take you."

I paused, pulling my mouth from her neck. "Oh? And, my sweet Tessa," I hissed as I traced a trail down to her nipples, provoking her to arch her back and suck in a sharp breath, "exactly *how* would that be?" I lifted my head and raised an eyebrow at her, giving her my best arrogant smartass smirk— just for good measure.

"This is our one and only night together, and I am not looking for sweet love," she said, her voice dropping, suddenly sounding unsure. Naïve even.

"So," I teased, "let me get this straight. You don't want me to make love to you? You want me to fuck you. HARD?" The thought of what she was asking provoked another bead to moisten the tip of my cock, and my voice hitched on *hard*. I had no words, and even if I did, none would come, so I only nodded.

Tessa took my assent eagerly and arched her back, aggressively pressing her most private parts into my already rigid and jerking cock. I slid my hands down her beautiful, firm calves, tossing them on my hips and up over my ass. *Oh my God, Tessa, my sweet, beautiful Tessa.* I drilled with intent against her scantily-sheathed apex, grinding hard against her before nestling my cock quietly on her dripping wet sex.

"See, I knew it!" I growled huskily into her ear. "I knew you'd be up for the kink, the lewd fucking lascivious shit I'm into. You don't know what you've asked for. I'm going to fuck you until I have to leave, and you will come so hard you won't be able to walk well into next week." I grinned arrogantly at her, and she smirked back. "You won't be able to think of anyone but me, the entire time I'm gone."

Her eyes twinkled and widened in anticipation as my mouth descended on hers for another soul-wrenching, cock-hardening, pussy-drenching kiss that curled our toes. I grabbed the hem of her camisole, which had already migrated up her midriff, rolling it into a makeshift blindfold that I placed over her eyes.

I sat back on my heels, admiring… no, indulging in the perfection and beauty of Tessa's planes and curves that molded to form the body of a goddess. I'd never really seen *her* for her. Sure, I'd obviously thought she was fucking sexy as hell, but recognizing her beautiful imperfections as jaw-dropping, stunningly beautiful… well, no.

Sure, I wanted to do right by Pallavi and Suri; it was why I was leaving this—as Ari put it—one in a million, unique woman. But he was right; she was special, and even if I'd already chosen Pallavi over Tessa, I didn't want to give her up completely either.

I reached down, and the slightest touch of my rough hand against her inner thigh made her shudder with anticipation. There was no way I'd leave her dissatisfied. I reached down and, with a swift tug, tore her sheer panties off.

My engorged cock jerked and jounced at the sight of her bare pussy, glistening with her juices in the dim light.

"God, Tessa, these are so fucking wet." I held the lace to my nose and inhaled deeply. "I cannot get enough of you. I love the way you smell." My words provoked a soft moan from her berry-red lips. *I can't wait to see what sound she'll make after this...*

I positioned my thighs, one between her legs and one farther up the bed, raising her hands above her head as I did. I swooped down for a kiss, then tied her hands together with the remnants of her barely-there panties. The darkest crimson blush caressed Tessa's cheeks, and her breathing came in short, uneven pants.

"You're so beautiful, Tessa; painfully, sinfully so. Do you have any idea the depth of my desire for you?" I lowered myself so my chest threatened to tease her nipples. Being this close without giving in to touch goose-bumped us both. I whispered in her ear, my passion-driven voice a low, husky growl, "Can you imagine how long I've ached to feel your hot, wet pussy around my cock? You have no idea what this means to me, or, since I've met you, how many nights I've lain awake in bed, needing to make you mine. Imagining how to make this happen, what I'd do to you. How you'd look tied up; how sweet your begging would sound; the readiness of your sex; how you'd taste. Jeezus, Tessa! What have you done to me? Will I ever be able to get over you?" My voice faltered, for confessing things aloud that I'd only ever admitted to the deepest regions of myself.

I sat back on my heels to admire my sweet Tessa one last time before I made her mine. I moved to gain access to her beautiful, smooth pussy. My breath teased her most sensitive spot as my hands moved. With one, I tormented her nipple, gently pulling and rolling it between my thumb and forefinger.

With the other, I gripped her hip firmly, possessing what was mine.

My desire surged through my fingertips; hers gushed, revealing her readiness for me. Finally, I couldn't hold back any longer. My mouth dove into her slick folds, drinking of her juices, kissing and sucking, plundering and fucking her with my tongue. Tessa fought her bonds, arched her back, and thrashed her head. Her raging need fed my own desire. I refocused my assault on her clit, lashing and flicking it as I expertly drove two fingers into her honey—and massaged and teased her g-spot until I could feel her muscles tightening. *I have to… I can't wait, Beautiful…*

In less than a second, I released my cock from its fabric prison and drove deeply into her, my nuts settling against her hot sex. I stifled the frenzied cry that was ripped from Tessa's lips, fueled by unrestrained emotion. The honey from her sex smeared across our lips and co-mingled between our tongues; a sweet and salty, heady concoction that threatened to make me come before I wanted to.

I raised my lips from hers, but with her emerald green eyes hidden, I couldn't find the validation I needed, so I ripped the blindfold off and double-banded her wrists.

"I need to see you, Tessa. I need to see your eyes when I come." I snarled my demand, my voice harsh with restraint and foreign to my own ears. My cock—the engorged bastard— twitched and sent Tessa's hips into mine powerfully as her back arched from the deep sensation.

"You feel so good. Oh my God, Noah. I just had…" Tessa panted and searched for the breath to express… "I had NO IDEA it would be like this with you."

"I did," I croaked. "I knew it from the moment our souls collided, and our bodies entwined together so perfectly. I knew you would do this to me." The vulnerability she evoked in me left me feeling exposed, and I looked away.

I withdrew from her completely and plunged back into her, methodically circling my hips and grazing her g-spot, before slowly pulling out and slamming back into her depths. Tessa countered each thrust, time and time again. She was beautiful to behold, perspiration dampening her flushed skin, her eyes hooded with passion, her lips slightly parted as she raked in shallow, uneven breaths.

Every time I slowly, deliberately, and with agonizing luxury, withdrew to my cock-tip, and then crammed my raging, torrid length root-deep into her, she broke before my eyes. Seeing her like this was painful, flattering, and would haunt me forever. I rutted into her with measured ferocity and withdrew with leisurely ease. My body may have been fucking her like she'd asked for—like we'd both needed—but my eyes made love to hers, never once looking away, demanding the truth from her, seeking her vulnerability and imploring her to stay in my life no matter what.

Our orgasms both built at an excruciating pace; only my restraint and experience delayed our simultaneous release.

"Tess…Ahhh… I can't any longer. I can't…" I garbled, unhinged, barely hanging on. I sat fully upright on my knees, and with both hands, yanked her hips up so only her shoulder blades remained on the bed. I powered into her lustily and pulled her to meet each of my thrusts—finally, she couldn't hold on any longer, though I struggled to hold off, as I felt the first of her orgasmic waves clench around me.

"Goddamn it—look at me!" I growled. *Fuck, Tess! I HAVE to see your eyes…*

She obeyed, opening her eyes in time for me to see her shatter under me. It was my undoing. I fractured into a million pieces above her as I exploded deep inside her soft, undulating pussy, her waves milking my hot seed from me.

I LOVE THIS WOMAN.

The realization hit me hard, but there was no way anyone could share such a crippling, soul-shattering climax unless the heart was involved. Waves of doubt about leaving, about going to see Pallavi entered my mind, and I forcefully pushed them out. *Suri, it's all for Suri.*

I collapsed onto my forearms, supporting my weight on either side of her. Reaching up, I yanked the lace panties from Tessa's wrists, and immediately, they enveloped me in a loving hug. It was undeniable what we'd shared was intense, and I could see in her eyes it had affected her too I knew she loved me if for no other reason than the silent tears that slipped from the corners of her eyes. I lay my chest on hers.

"Tessa…"

"Noah."

"I can't even describe what you've done to me."
There's so much more I want to say… but the words evaded me.

"I know. Me either."

I raised myself up and kissed her with all the adoration and love I felt. It was a sensual, languid kiss, unhurried and surreal, especially knowing that what we'd just shared would be the only time I'd ever feel that with her… with anyone.

I sat back on my heels, still buried inside her, breathless and grasping for any viable reason other than selfish love that would keep me here and away from my daughter. I watched Tessa, and the emotions that flitted across her face, languorous at first, then a soft peace washed over her, and then almost suddenly, a ridiculous, cat-got-the-mouse, shit-eating grin from spread across her face.

I chuckled. "Looks like I did something right." I winked at her and flashed her my arrogant, cocky-ass smirk. I could feel myself swell to ramrod hardness in her again… *God, what this woman does to me!*

"Maybe…" she cooed as she squeezed the soft walls of her desire so that it ran ripples along my already heated and ready-to-go-again cock.

Damn you, woman! I strained, clenching my teeth, doing everything I could to transfer the balance of power in my direction. "Hmm," I growled huskily, "Well, if you're not too sure, then maybe I should rectify that?" I pulled out, and with smooth and practiced movement, flipped Tessa so she lay face down under me. My hands gripped her hipbones and snapped her up on her knees before me, ass high in the air. With no prelude, I ran my cock-head through her hot, wet folds and crammed into her full to the hilt again, smacking her ass for good measure. "I still need to make good on my promise that you won't be able to walk or forget me while I'm gone." I grabbed the tendrils of hair at the base of her neck, wrapping them around one fist as I placed the other on her shoulder. I began another calculated assault—one of many—before we were both too spent to move.

Hours later, I lay wrapped in a cocoon of sweat-dampened sheets, my arms cuddling her, my mind drifting between reality and dreams. *I love you, Tessa.* "I love you." Three little words fell from my lips in a sleepy confession, not one I'm even sure she heard, but one I felt she needed to hear.

"Babe, there's someone at the door." The soft purr tickled my ear and all of my senses became aware of Tessa, her smell, her feel, and especially her ass against my growing erection as I held her captive in a strong, possessive hug. "It's only 0945."

Mmm... morning sex. There's plenty of time. I thrust my hard dick powerfully against her ass cheeks. *Wait! Holy Fuck!* "9:45?! Oh, my God, let me up!" I moved Tessa aside and bounded out of bed. Grabbing my boxer-briefs, I ran across the room, my toe snagging in the discarded clothes on the floor and nearly tripping me. Upon reaching the door, I threw it open.

Dirk stood there, disheveled, groggy, and looking all the worse for wear. "Oh, this is great. You have got to be fucking kidding me. Good thing I decided to check on your sorry ass—you should've been on the 0935 transport to the airport! Your flight is at 1145 and you're supposed to arrive there two hours early to clear customs and get weighed in." He pushed past me. "Damnit, Noah! Don't just stand there. You're going to blow your ticket... get the fuck ready. You're already late!"

I needed no other prodding; I sprang into action, swooping up my jeans from the floor. *What the fuck am I supposed to do with this thing? Fuck!* I uncomfortably shoved my hard dick in my pants and tried to get the fly closed. I glanced at Tessa. A smirk now graced her lips.

"What can I do to help?"

"Please help me find my shirt and shoes. *Fuck*," I grumbled, "I can't find shit in here."

She slid from the bed, grabbed her robe and began sorting through the discarded clothing we'd scattered across the floor last night. She held out the items I needed, and I gave her a quick hug as I took them, throwing them on.

"Just breathe," she soothed with a sweet smile. "The plane isn't going to leave without you, and they never leave on time anyway."

I knew she was trying to calm my nerves, but it did shit to help me feel calm. "Shit, Tessa, I have less than five minutes if I want to catch the 0955 bus, which is NEVER going to happen… I still have to run back to the barracks and get my shit packed." I was panicked, and after I spoke, I looked at her to make sure she didn't take it as roughly as it sounded. Thankfully, she looked unperturbed, so I grabbed my jacket, zipped it and ran a hand through my unruly hair. I nearly made it out the door…*TESSA!* I paused, and upon turning, grabbed her arm. I pulled her against me for a heart-fluttering, dick-hardening kiss.

"No matter what happens, you have part of my heart and soul forever. Last night meant more to me than even I could've imagined. You've done something to me. *Permanently.* I have A LOT to think about. I just wanted you to know that before I leave today." I smiled at her, "Besides, you have more important things to worry about, like a deployment to Turkey." I squeezed her, and in spite of the time, found it hard to let her go.

Tessa nuzzled into my chest. She looked up into my weary blue eyes with her big green ones. Her mouth opened as though to say something, but that look, the look she gave me, pierced straight into my soul.

"All I have to say is… thanks for last night." Her voice cracked, and I could see she was struggling not to cry. "I wish you the best of luck, Noah, and the rest…" she paused and offered me a sad smile, "how I feel just doesn't matter, because you've already bought your tickets."

I squeezed her again and just stood there, willing myself to go but unable to move through the door.

"Noah—now! You've got to go!" The urgency in Dirk's voice resonated with me. I broke our embrace and strode toward the still open door. Dirk had already started down the hall.

I made it through the door, knowing I should be running after Dirk, but my feet wouldn't move. There was still so much to say. I wanted to tell her I never meant to hurt her, and Suri, not Pallavi was my reason for going. I wanted to tell her I didn't want for this to be goodbye… but I felt it. Looking at her as she turned back and just stood there staring at me in the middle of the hallway, I could see that she felt it was our final goodbye too. I scrubbed my hands over my face, through my mess of hair and swiped angrily at the renegade tears my traitorous eyes released.

Then, the door CLOSED.

This is it. It's over. I've lost her… I swiped at the tears that now flowed, freely and without shame, down my cheeks. *No, fuck that!*

I walked the two steps to her door and knocked heavily. I had no idea what I'd say or do, but I just *had* to see her again. Tessa opened the door and after the shock registered that it was me, she flung herself into my arms. My strong arms encircled her, and the feeling that for as long as I held her, I had her… had me forgetting about the bus I should be catching.

I looked into those emerald eyes of hers, and their depths pulled me in just like her red locks sucked my hands into their waves. I laid a no-holds-barred kiss on her that weakened both our knees.

How? How can her kiss do this to me? Fear—fear of losing her, fear of having made a wrong choice, fear that I might never feel this way again—registered in my expression, and when our lips parted, I know that's all she saw looking back at her.

She quickly kissed me, then pushed me, encouraging me to leave as she shut the door on me.

"Tessa!" The most grieved, insecure and wounded voice escaped past my lips—causing Tessa to freeze in her tracks. She reopened the door a crack. I just stood there in yesterday's wrinkled clothes, emotionally naked, unashamed and scared. I smiled sheepishly and shrugged. Tessa blew me a final kiss. Only the closing door broke the energy and connection passing between us.

The sound of the door clicking in its jamb resonated deeply in me. I turned and ran toward the stairwell that led to my trip into the unknown. Tormented tears rolled down my cheeks. More than one door had just closed.

Vexed

-ONE-

I stowed my backpack under the seat in front of me, sat back and glanced at my watch: 1138. It blew my mind that I'd made it here on time, considering I'd left Tessa's room fewer than two hours ago. I put my headphones on, closed my eyes and settled back into my first-class seat. Tessa and her irresistible… *everything,* drifted into my mind. *Damnit, fucker. Stop! You ended it with her…* I should've been thinking about Pallavi and Suri, but that woman had cast a serious spell on me.

I'd arrived at the airport after they started boarding for check in and had casually asked at the check-in counter if there was any way for a free seat upgrade. The counter attendant had only met my eyes once before looking down. She clicked away on her keyboard, working her magic. Before I'd known it, my rear seat had been changed to first class and I had the new tickets in my paws. I opened my eyes, taking in the posh leather seats that surrounded mine and grinned. *Things are definitely improving from this morning.* Again, images of Tessa's arms around my neck, her body molded against me, and her lips searching mine… flooded into my head. I shook it away, adamant that she'd leave me in peace.

"Anything I can get you, sir?"

I dragged my gaze up to the source of the voice and found a tall but not overly attractive flight attendant looking expectantly at me.

"Double Jack & Coke please." *Fuck.* Now I was ordering what Tessa liked and had gotten me hooked on. "Make it a triple," I groused with a heavy sigh.

She looked shocked but replied with an obligatory, "I'll be right back, sir."

I loved that my upgrade included free drinks, although I bet there was a cap—*fuck, I bet I already owe her for a shot…or two.*

"Excuse me, but 'ey believe 'ye are in my seat."

I looked up and the attractive middle-aged Icelandic woman with long, wavy dark hair, proffered her ticket in my direction.

"You can have mine," I nodded to the seat beside me.

"'Ey would prefer *my* window seat." She placed her hands on her hips and waited, holding up the stragglers who had boarded behind her.

I stowed my tray, up-righted my seat, grabbed my pack and edged past her, barely allowing the clearance she needed to squeeze by.

"Thank 'ye," she grumbled through clenched teeth as she brushed past me.

Fucking great… I have over twenty hours. I sure hope I get a new seat-neighbor at Heathrow. I dropped my pack and kicked it under the seat in front of me, reclined my seat, turned up my CD player and closed my eyes.

"Where are 'ye heading?"

Seriously? Now she wants to be fucking chummy? "St. John's."

"Obviously not Newfoundland," she said with a confused pause, "since we're headed off to London 'ey?"

"St. John's—the British Caribbean island." My voice was deadpan. "You're getting off in London?" I sounded hopeful.

Just then, the pre-flight safety speech—use the seat as a floatation device, pull our oxygen masks down in case of emergency, these are the exit doors, yada yada— interrupted us. It was the usual, and I've flown so much that I listened with half an ear. My mind shifted to Tessa. My last morning with her, how perfect it was… *God, I loved the way her pussy hugged my cock, her warmth, her smell, the mewing sound she made*—my dick twitched thinking about it. *Damnit,* I chided myself, *I've got to stop thinking about her!* As if this were even possible.

The flight attendant had finished her safety speech, checked and secured all overhead compartments, and buckled into her seat a few rows from me at the front of the cabin.

"Prepare for takeoff," the captain's voice crackled over the plane's intercom. "Please make sure your seats are in the upright position, tray tables are properly stowed, and all electronics are turned off," the intercom clicked off and I watched the attendant hook her mic on the wall beside where she was belted in.

Here I come, Suri! As the plane screamed down the runway, pressure forced my back and head into my seat with a familiarity I'd missed. *Man, I love flying.*

"Miami."

Fuck! My attention was immediately redirected to the Icelander beside me. "What?" I asked with a tinge of annoyance.

"My da'. You asked me where 'ey was headed. He passed and 'ey am headed home to Miami to see my mam and sisters."

"Sorry for your loss." I shifted my weight and angled myself away from her slightly—trying to give her the hint that I wasn't a big talker. I had just turned my damn music up again…

"'Ey have been to St. John's, it is a beautiful place 'ey." I refused to take her bait, so she tried again. "Ye' know, 'ye have to take a ferry from St. Thomas to St. John's 'ey?"

"I'm taking a water taxi. My daughter and wife," I choked on the lie, "are meeting me on the docks." *What the…? Why was that so hard to get out? I mean, that is why I am headed here, right? To solidify things and plan a future with Vi?*

"Ahh, 'ye are on a leisure visit then?" she commented as though her cogs were turning. "So 'ye are stationed here in Keflavik 'ey?"

"Yes. We do long distance and connect whenever her modeling career allows."

"So, 'ye are living like a high-roller huh? 'Ey was wondering how 'ye could afford first class on a military salary…"

I interrupted, building on the lie I was fabricating… *fuck it.* "Yeah, she's my sugar momma. She pays for everything." I chuckled. "I just service her real-good every few months, and I get whatever I want."

The look on her face was priceless. She closed her gaping jaws, "So, —and excuse my frankness—but 'ye are sayin' 'ye get paid for 'ye services?" Her eyes practically bugged out of her head.

"We're married. It's what she signed up for. She wants my cock, and I want her money." A deep belly laugh erupted from deep within me. I'd needed this cathartic release after the morning I'd had with Tessa.

"Well," she narrowed her eyes shrewdly at me, "'ey never."

"Then don't," I said, still laughing.

She didn't bother me for the whole rest of the flight.

-TWO-

I glanced at my watch—just enough time to give Dirk a call before boarding my flight from Miami to St. Thomas. I dialed the digits on the public phone, one in a long line of phones in stark cubbies along the airport terminal's wall.

"Keflavik Base Security, main office, Petty Officer Cordet."

"Hey, Kelly. It's Garren."

"Hey, Noah. So you already miss us, huh?" she joked good-naturedly, and I could envision a sarcastic look gracing her pleasant features. If my life weren't already such a mess chick-wise, I could surely see myself trying to hit that at some point; we were both second class petty officers, so it would've been an easy, no hassle affair.

"I just wanted to hear your laugh one last time…"

She interrupted me, "Sure you did, Romeo. I'll go get Archibladt for ya."

I could hear her convey to someone in the office that I was on the line and ask where Dirk was. Shortly after, his rambunctious laughter rolled through the receiver, and soon, several other people in the vicinity of the phone were cracking up. Just one of the many reasons I kept Dirk around as a good friend; he was consistently upbeat and fun to be around.

"Hey ya, man, what's 'sup?" I opened my mouth, but he continued, "It can't be good if you're already callin' me. What's it been, only most of a day?" He laughed, and I heard more jabs thrown my way in the background

Damn peanut gallery! "Yeah, I'm at the end of my layover in Miami, then have just under a three-hour flight, but I just…"

He interrupted again, "But you just wanted to…"

"Listen, fucker! It's not like it's easy calling you, but who else am I going to talk to? Who else can give me advice from the perspective you can? No one else knows the shit I've been dealing with, except you."

"*Jeezus,* man, what's eating you up? Vi? Tess?"

I sighed heavily. "How is she? I mean, you've seen her right? Since I left?"

"Yeah, I mean I guess so, but shouldn't your mind be on Vi? I mean, why are you all cracked out on a fiery red-head when you have a sexy Middle Eastern model waiting to suck your dick?" He paused, and I pictured him shrugging his shoulders and shaking his head like he always did when we'd had this conversation—Pallavi vs. Tessa—in the past. "From what Sam said, that Ari fucker invited the two of them with his flight crew to go sightseeing for the day, but I didn't see her until later that night, when I stopped by, after they'd gotten back."

Fucking Ari! Already making a play, and her sheets still smell of me. Fucker. "How was she?"

"She was fucking tired, Noah; pretty much a zombie slogging around. Honestly, she's taking this shit pretty hard, but I still don't see why you care. You ended it with her, right? So, suck it up, focus on the mission at hand—seeing if there's a future with Vi at your side, along with Suri. You don't need to be doubting yourself." he chuckled uncomfortably. "You're already in this too far, man, and I don't think Tess is much of an option right now."

"I know. It's just…fuck, Dirk! I can't get her out of my head. Every time my mind quiets for a second, there she is! I can't stop thinking about her." My voice grated with all my pent-up emotion. "I've thought about 'what if' with Vi for so long; dreamt for so many years of a future with her and me raising Suri," my voice cracked, "but lately, all I'm doing is dreaming about Tess! I mean, my mind goes to her anytime I'm not talking with someone or singing song lyrics in my head…seriously. I mean, every time I get any shut-eye, bam! There she is with her raspberry mouth, fiery locks and emerald eyes… and those tits…" I set the receiver down and scrubbed my palms over my face, then combed them through my hair.

"You there, buddy? Hello?"

"Yeah, I'm here. I just needed a sec."

"Well, Noah, the way I see it is this,"

The airport intercom for Delta crackled overhead, "Flight 8906 with direct service from Miami to St. Thomas is pre-boarding all passengers with children or who need assistance."

"Sorry, my flight is getting ready to board."

"Need me to let you go?"

"In a sec Dirk, you were saying the way you see it is…?"

"Oh yeah, right. Well, the way I see it is this: Tess is old news. At least, she'd better be; you'd best get her out of your head, cause she's a fucking mess. And I mean, I know you don't want to hear it, but she's hurting real bad."

It was as though he took the knife in my chest and drove it in deeper, twisting it slowly back and forth as he sunk it in.

"Now Vi, she's today's news. Sure, you have a past with her, but you've never been able to get her out of your head either. I mean, you've told me that she's the reason that you started jumping…" Dirk lowered his voice, "from pussy to pussy. Right? I mean correct me if I'm wrong, but she started you on this path of searching for the next chick like her… right?"

I nodded. Everything he was saying made perfect sense. I knew I'd been on the hunt for a woman who lived up to my memory of Pallavi, and here I was, going to actually *see her. What's the fuck's wrong with me?* "You're right."

"Damn straight I'm right! Jeezus, Noah, you have a kid with her, and she's a goddamn *MODEL*. Doesn't sound like Tess holds a candle to her."

That's where he's wrong.

"Flight 8906 with direct service from Miami to St. Thomas will begin boarding First Class rows 1-10."

"Sounds like you need to go. Besides, I'm sure your credit card company has to be loving you right about now?"

I looked at my watch—*fuck*—yeah, this call was going to cost me a pretty penny. "Wait. There's something you should know."

"Unless it will change the course you're on, man—you need to just let it go."

"Well, it does. Remember me telling you about the one girl that got away? The only girl who's ever used me for sex," I rubbed the back of my neck and switched the phone receiver to my other ear.

"Yeah, but, Noah... I don't see what that has to do with anything? *Jeezus fuck*! Did you just run into her at the airport?"

I laughed. "No, no... nothing like that, but we have met since that night in Wazzu..." I took a slow, deep breath. I should've told him everything, long before now. After all, he was my best friend in Keflavik.

"What the fuck? When?"

"Dirk, man, it's Tess."

"No. Fucking. Way!"

"Yeah," I hurried, continuing before he could condemn me. "The reason I was so drawn to Tessa at first was because she resembled the girl that night. Then, when I realized it was her—she didn't know who I was—so I've let the sleeping bear lie."

"Jeezus, Noah."

"I know."

"Well, if I'd known your draw to Tess was the cosmic one you've always spoken of… my advice probably wouldn't have been the same."

"I know. Sorry I've lied, but the whole thing is so fucking messed up."

"Hey, man, it's your business. But now, really, the only thing you can do is move forward, cause Tessa sure as fuck isn't getting over what you've done to her—making her second rung to your *maybe* with Vi."

I nodded, even though he couldn't see me.

"You've been waiting for this chance, so forget Tessa. There sure as hell isn't a maybe with her, so explore your options with Vi. I mean, it *is* what you've wanted—actually waited for—all these years, right?"

"Yeah, man…"

The airport intercom interrupted, "Flight 8906 with direct service from Miami to St. Thomas is now boarding all first class rows."

"Thanks, Dirk, I know you're right. I just needed to hear it, I guess."

"Sure thing—now go hit that fine-ass pussy!"

We both laughed, said our goodbyes and hung up. I sat there for a second, my forehead in my hands, forcing Tessa— the red-headed siren—out of my thoughts. *Hopefully, for good.* I grabbed my backpack and ticket and proceeded to the gate.

Tina Maurine

-THREE-

I stepped off the private water taxi Pallavi had arranged for me. The St. Thomas Water Taxi Co. had picked me up from the Cyril E. King Airport in a private luxury SUV transport that had taken me to the east end of Saint Thomas where their boats were moored at the Sapphire Bay Marina. Pallavi had thought of everything. She'd even had them stock my favorites for the ride to the marina—Tanqueray and cigarettes—although I no longer smoked and now drank bourbon, not gin.

I looked around. Glancing at my watch, I couldn't make heads or tails of how long I'd been last in bed, since the time here was hours ahead of Iceland, and I felt pretty jet-lagged from the more than twenty-three-hour adventure—counting this taxi ride—I'd been on. *Jeezus it's fucking hot and not even eight am.* Sweat rolled down the spinal valley of my muscled back and began to dampen the waistband of my board shorts.

"Is anyone meeting you here?"

I turned around and looked at the young captain's assistant who was casting off the lines from the dock. "I don't really know."

He nodded to the shop down the dirt road from the pier. "They open soon for good breakfast."

"Thanks." I saluted him good-bye as he waved, and then I redirected my attention to the unoccupied pier, which, to my surprise, was no longer empty. An exotic woman, tall, yet still feminine in stature with long, wavy black hair was heading my way. As she neared me, I saw she wore it partially up, with tendrils framing her face. Her white bikini contrasted strikingly with her bronze tan. A sheer sarong was slung low on her hips and tied off-center in front, a playful accessory, as were the beaded necklaces, bracelets and anklets she wore.

"Ya Habibi." She greeted me 'My Love' as she always had, walking toward me with open arms.

"Hiya, gorgeous!"

She folded into my arms, her skin soft and silken against my rough fingertips. I ran lines up and down her back, and she shivered. Looking up at me, her warm, chestnut eyes sparkled.

"Wahashtini, Ya Habibi."

I stiffened. "I've missed you too." *But do I still love her?* The question slammed into my heart, pushing a not so distant memory of Tessa forward. *Fuck.* I skipped the whole *'I love you'* notion and complimentary endearments that went with it and opted for a safer approach. "I'm glad I'm finally here."

"Me too." With her soft admission, she lifted her chin and pulled my head down to her meet her lips. Mine responded to hers, soft and yielding, but hers took charge of our kiss. This first kiss.

She entwined the fingers of her other hand in the hair at the nape of my neck, driving my head, steering the kiss, and encouraging me to give myself over to her. I tried. Her soft, pouty lips were sexy as fuck, and she kissed me with pent-up passion that came close to matching the fervor that I'd felt in Iceland with… *FUCK!* I killed that thought dead in its tracks.

I pulled her heavy, full chest into mine as I encircled her waist. I wove my fingers in her long tresses, which I'd released from their clasp, and drove my tongue into her mouth—demanding, seeking, hoping to push any last trace of *her* from my conscious mind. The last thing I needed was to feel guilty that I was kissing this woman, the mother of my child. Pallavi folded into me, pressing herself tighter against me than I thought possible, and into my traitorous cock, which was already swelling with desire. She nipped and sucked my lips, and I teased hers, while our kiss only deepened. The cacophony of sounds that met my ears signaled the dockside shops opening, but they didn't faze me; however, her sly hand finding my hard erection did. I pulled back, abruptly ending the kiss.

"Vi."

"He wants me. I knew he needed me still." She grabbed a handful of my cock and gently squeezed. "I've needed him too." She removed her hand from the front of my shorts and ran her index finger over my lip, then along my jawline where a dark five 'o-clock shadow had already grown in.

I reached up and gently took her hand in mine, bringing it down to my side. She backed up until we stood side by side, holding hands and looking at the newly-opened dockside shops and restaurants.

I pointed to the small café the captain's assistant had told me was good. "When I got in, they recommended we grab breakfast there."

She sighed heavily, then recovered with a smile. "Sure, Ya Habibi, anything for you."

We walked hand in hand to a small, hole-in-the-wall that was tastefully decorated in tropical décor. A pretty young brunette greeted us cheerily. "Morning! Please sit anywhere you'd like." She handed us the short menus and gestured with a wide sweeping motion of her hands for us to take a seat anywhere. "They're all open. You beat the crowds by getting up so early."

"Yes, hun, we did." Pallavi gave her a suggestive raised eyebrow and winked.

"Or maybe you're just getting in?" The hostesses winked back suggestively and giggled.

We took our seats at a small two-person table that overlooked the ocean. I held my menu, my wrists resting on the table, distractedly flipping it from side to side, hoping one of the menu choices would stand out to me. Pallavi reached out and placed her hand on mine. I drew it back.

"Ya Habibi?"

"Don't '*My Love*' me. I thought you'd remember from the last time you did this in New York, that sexual innuendos and alluding to our sex life to perfect strangers… *Fuck,* Vi, it makes me uncomfortable as hell." I was pissed, and my tone was probably shorter and harsher than I'd intended.

Immediately, and I mean as though a fucking switch had been flipped, Pallavi turned on the waterworks. Tears streamed down her cheeks, complete with a quivering bottom lip. "You're so mad at me, Noah, my love? Why? What did I do that was so wrong? All I said was that we'd gotten up early…"

I cut her off. "It's not what you said, it's all the bullshit winking and eyebrow crap you *always* do. It's like you want people to always think we just came from fucking our brains out."

"Well, by tomorrow this time, we will have." She said it softly as she stared down at her menu, playing with the separating corner of the laminated page.

"Oh? You think so, huh?"

"Ya Habibi, what happened to us? Aren't you here to make this work? Isn't this what you want?" Her usual confident, and arrogant alto wavered.

I shrugged. "Of course, I have that hope." I looked from her mesmerizing brown pools back down to my menu.

The waitress stopped by our table just then and took first my order—a fresh shrimp breakfast burrito with eggs, bacon, gruyere cheese, avocado and salsa, with a side of home fries and coffee—and then Pallavi's no sugar, no fat Caramel Mocha and egg whites. Plain. Then I thanked her, and she left us to our awkwardness.

Do I still want life plain? Stripped of all the sugar and fat—of all the good things that make life more satisfying and pleasurable? I wasn't so sure anymore. It was looking more and more like my tastes had changed.

"Ana Bahebak."

"How can you still say you love me?"

"Because I do. Ya habib alby. Ya rouhi."

"Damn it, Vi," I said, exasperated. "My Gulf Arabic isn't as strong as it used to be. English would help me a lot. It would keep us from having any miscommunication."

"Ya Amar," she caught herself and looked as though she were chastising herself inwardly. "My moon, I just had said that you're the love of my heart. You are my soul."

My shoulders slumped. *What am I doing here?*

She continued, seemingly unfazed by my carriage and attitude, "So, for me, it is easy to say that I still love you, because it is complete, eternal love. Don't you still love me?"

I didn't want to get into all this here, not even thirty minutes off the boat. "Vi, let's just say I'm trying to figure everything out."

But NO! That wasn't good enough for her. "You're trying to figure things out? Couldn't you have done that over the phone?" Her Middle Eastern accent grew thick now that she wasn't getting her way.

"Vi, when I came home that morning to your flat, and *your husband* was there, in the middle of your floor, dripping wet from the rain…FUCK, Vi! You didn't say anything to me! How could you not say anything? How did you just let me walk out of your life after our time in Kuwait, and how hard we'd fought to be together?"

Fuck this. I took a deep, cleansing breath, and in an even tone asked the most important question I had. "Where's Suri? I was really looking forward to meeting my daughter."

Pallavi continued to roll the corner of the menu that the waitress had mistakenly left after taking our order.

"Where is she, Vi?"

"She's with her nanny, Leah, and my assistant Rue. I thought since I had a shoot earlier at dawn today, I'd come alone. Was that not okay?"

"When will I see her?"

"Ya Habibi," she said, recovering her sugary-sweet tone, "I have a whole day planned for us. I have a photo shoot on a Double D yacht, the Santa Maria. Antoine de Saint Luxevoiné, the artistic director, chartered it for us to stay on tonight with the shoot staff. There's five rooms and wait staff. It should be fun for you. I promise. Won't you please focus on just us? Won't you please give this a valiant try?" She reached out for my hand, and this time, I let her take it. "Trust me, there will be plenty of time to see her. Focus on us first, okay?"

-FOUR-

The advice from the water taxi staff had been spot on. Breakfast had been the bomb. I'd eaten all of mine and the rest that Pallavi hadn't been able to finish… no wonder she was as slim as she was. After our rough start, we were moving in the right direction. The conversation at breakfast had been light-hearted and had mostly centered around her latest travels in the Caribbean and Gulf Coast. We'd fallen into a comfortable rhythm of touching and flirting, and had held hands on the way back to her hotel. It had nearly felt like old times; hell, when that guy Antonine embraced her in the lobby, I'd even had a pang of jealousy I'd not been expecting.

Now, here I sat on the middle deck of the three, on a massive 155-foot luxury yacht, watching Pallavi do her thing. The yacht was cruising, and her hair blew behind her. She was quite the enchantress, now topless, holding her chest—barely—with one hand as she put the other to her hair, or over her mouth, across her abdomen. She was obviously a pro and listened to and worked well with the photographer. She wore her sultry eyes while she posed—click, then her playful, laughing face, pose—click. She went through the whole gamut of expressions in a matter of minutes. I hadn't really seen her doing her thing before, since the time we'd spent together years ago had been about just the two of us. She'd taken off work and we'd pretty much vacationed in bed. I smiled thinking about how our time together in New York had been so perfect. I stretched out on the crisp white sun lounge, yawned and put my hands behind my head. *Ahhh, this is the life. I could definitely get used to this.*

"You should wear that more often, it suits you." Her hair grazed my chest as she bent down to kiss me. "It's so nice to see you smiling."

I opened my eyes to a skimpily-clad bronze frame standing over me.

"Ah, and here I thought you were talking about my stylish board shorts." I laughed, pulling her thighs to me and kissed her full lips again as she bent over. She tasted of Cristal and strawberries, both of which I planned to taste off her body later in our suite. Tessa's perfect athletic, petite little frame popped into my head, and I felt the blood surge into my dick.

"Looks like he wants a kiss too," she giggled and began to trail kisses down my abdomen. *Damn it, Tess! Get the fuck out!* I pushed her from my mind, and although she left, she was never far away.

Pallavi placed her knee between my thighs and lowered herself onto my body, her full breasts overflowing from the small triangles that were there more for decoration than practicality. Her lips dragged languorous kisses across my collarbones and up to the sensitized spot on my neck that drove me crazy. *Fuck it. It doesn't matter…* I wove my strong fingers into her shiny hair, taking command of the kiss. My tongue darted and explored her mouth, savoring its sweetness. My lips danced with hers before I mouth fucked her.

"Jeezus, Vi," I huskily growled, "I want you." To emphasize this, I thrust upward strongly—swallowing the gasp on her lips.

My free hand roughly grabbed her firm ass, pulling her powerfully into my engorged cock. Somewhere in the distance, I faintly heard, "Let's give them some privacy. Take lunch." Bodies walked past us, and now all I heard as the background music to our labored breaths were the waves and the yacht's powerful engine.

Wrapping my muscular arm around her tiny waist, I swiftly rolled her onto her back. "Tell me," I growled throatily, "tell me what you want me to do next, cause… *fuck*, Vi…" I paused to kiss her wanton mouth and ground my hard cock into her barely-clothed, moist apex. "I've waited so long for this…"

She placed her hands on my face, stilling me. Her honey-brown eyes shimmered with unshed tears, brimming with passion. "You. All I want," her voice caught in her throat, and she delicately cleared it. "All I have ever wanted is you."

"I don't have anything."

"We already have a daughter together. You don't need to worry. I won't run away again." She slid her hand from my face, down my back, into my waistband and gripped my ass, tugging me against her tightly. "I need to feel you in me, Noah." She wiggled beneath me, and my dick grew even harder, if that was possible. "More importantly, I need for you to feel me around you. For you to remember." She gyrated provocatively, and it worked.

I rotated slightly onto my side, and my hand pushed away the suggestion of fabric that she wore over her right breast. My mouth replaced it, aggressively sucking, kissing and nipping at it—each drawing a heated gasp from her. I cupped her swollen breast and massaged it. *God, I fucking love her tits!* I pressed my face between her full breasts and ran kisses along the inner crest of the left, which was pressed firmly against my right shoulder.

"Noah." A deprived whisper fell from her lips.

I snatched my name off them with a heated kiss. I drank her in. Before she could go on, I trailed my left hand from her breast, which I was still cupping, down her insanely flat abdomen, over her hip to the tie of her dainty suit bottom. I tugged it loose and stole the sharp intake of breath off her lips.

"You're mine," I growled. "All mine." I kissed her fervently as I slid my palm over her bare mound, my long middle finger sliding between her velvet folds. Finding her honeyed core, I coated both my middle and index finger with her slick juices and worked them through her folds, paying attention to her most sensitive bud. I worked circles around it and tweaked it with slight pinches and diminutive squeezes. Pallavi's back arched, and her warm chestnut eyes hooded. It nearly sent me over the edge, seeing her break like this before me.

My dick danced within the loose confines of my board shorts. He needed attention. NOW.

"Vi," I sighed in a pained, gravelly voice that sounded unfamiliar to my own ears, "I want you."

Her slender fingers found my nape and pulled my mouth to hers for a hot, deep kiss. "I'm yours."

It was the go-ahead I needed. I tugged on the strings of my shorts and ripped open my Velcro fly, releasing my cock with a heaviness that demanded immediate relief. Grabbing my dick firmly, I smeared the drips from my tip, over my head and pumped myself a couple of times. *Fuuuuck...* I quickly slipped a rubber on and angled myself over her, spreading her legs wide, and running my hot, throbbing cock through her juices, teasing her clit until I couldn't take it anymore. I snaked my right hand under her shoulder blade and grabbed her shoulder, cupping it—and drove into her hard—very hard.

My head shot back at the feeling of her pussy around me, and I drove into her with a feverish urgency. I pulled down on her shoulders with each brutal thrust. I was punishing her, making her take all that I had, and her flushed skin and the raking of her nails over my back showed me she loved it.

I pumped with abandon, gyrating my hips, withdrawing to my head and driving into her deeply, again and again, until I felt her arching her hips into me.

"Come for me," I commanded with a harshness I felt no remorse for, and she did, letting go of the last thread of restraint she'd been clinging to. I pounded into her twice more before I found my release. Her velvet pussy ran waves along my undulating cock, milking me until I was fully spent. I lowered my body onto hers and nuzzled into her neck as I breathed heavily. A million thoughts were running through my head, but there wasn't a single one I wanted to share with her.

I pulled out and stowed him away in my swim shorts, grabbing the linen towel that was wrapped around the bottle of Cristal and tossed it onto Pallavi's belly. She looked up at me. "Gee," she said softly, questioning me with eyes that were now piercing, no longer soft, "thanks, I guess?"

"I don't know, I thought maybe you might want to get yourself cleaned up and join the others for lunch," I stated matter-of-factly as I turned away from her and headed towards the inside sun-deck lounge.

"Noah?" A surprisingly timid voice quivered out my name. It caused me to pause and I turned around. Pallavi was tying her suit at her hip and looking after me, hope etched across her face.

I smiled and shrugged. "I'm gonna grab a cold one and find a satellite phone—I need to call and check on some stuff back in Keflavik." My smile garnered one from her, and I tossed out an obligatory, "Thanks, that was… fun," before I headed inside. I knew I was being a cold-hearted dick, but something deep down in me refused to care.

I nearly bumped into one of the Santa Maria's crew as I stepped through the sliding wall of windows. "Hey man, sorry. I was wondering where I could find a cold brewski and a phone. I need to make an international call for work."

The young blonde kid was maybe twenty-one or twenty-two and looked like a surfer. His hair was bleached on top and long, and he tossed his head to get his long bangs out of his eyes before nodding over to the stairs that led to the floor below. "There's a few different beers available. Genevieve is at

the bar making drinks now, and she can tell you what she's got.
I can bring you a phone there, too. I've just got to deliver a
message to Ms. Amrav. Is she outside?" He motioned to the
deck we'd just fucked out on.

"Yeah, Vi's out there. You might want to make sure
she's decent though before you head out." I cocked my
eyebrow and smirked arrogantly.

"Ohhh, ok. Sure thing. Thanks." He walked hesitantly
toward the slider, peering into the bright sunlight, then turned
to me chuckling. "Phew, looks like I'm in the clear. Thanks
again!"

I nodded. "Any time. You're bringing the phone?"

"Yes, sir, in just a minute." He strode confidently out
the door towards the fine piece of ass I'd just had.

*Fine piece of ass. What's wrong with me? Why am I
talking about her like she's a weekend trollop? Fuck! I need to
meet my daughter.*

I headed downstairs and took a seat at the bar, smiling
to the modeling crew who were seated around two low tables
with plush chairs pulled up to them. Several plates of tapas
were spread out around the table, littered between with many
more drinks. Behind the bar, an attractive, dark-skinned
woman with platinum blonde hair came over to me.

"What can I do for ya?" She smiled seductively, and
my dick twitched. *WHAT THE FUCK?*

"Well…" I cocked my brow, and then laughed. "Just
kidding. A beer. Dark if you have it."

"Coming up." She tossed her hair as she turned with the
empty pint glass in her hand and headed to the tap.

I grabbed a bowl of mixed pretzels and peanuts and
threw a few into my mouth. My thoughts immediately drifted
to Tessa. *I wonder what she's doing before she leaves for
Turkey? Bet she's with that opportunist, Ari. He'd better not*

think this means she's available… What the fuck am I saying? Technically she is—damn it! I shouldn't have broken it off with her before I knew how this would all play out. Have I done irreparable damage? Will she even take me back? Will she accept Suri?

"Sir. Sir?" I lifted my head and the long-haired kid from earlier was standing near me proffering the satellite phone.

"Thanks, man." I smiled and took the phone, then glanced to the bartender.

She came over and set my frothy, dark beer down. "What do I owe ya?"

"Not a thing. It's part of the yacht rental."

"Oh? Anything else come with the package deal?" Again, I smiled provocatively.

She laughed it off. "I am sure your every need can be met, sir." She smiled flirtatiously before turning heel.

"What the fuck is that all about?" I spun on my bar stool, and there stood Pallavi with her arms folded across her chest, looking pissed. She glared at me, and then hissed under her breath, "Did you really just fuck me, and now… not even five minutes later, you're flirting with the slut bartender?" She glowered at the platinum blonde mixologist who'd served me. "Are you planning to fuck her too? Before or after you'd planned on hooking up with me again?"

"Jeezus, Vi. Cool your heels. You're so off base it's ridiculous."

"Oh, so now I'm ridiculous?"

"Yeah," I nodded to her body. "Fuck, Vi. Just take a look at yourself in the mirror." I glanced over to the large mirror behind the bar counter.

Her eyes followed where I'd indicated, and she dropped her arms. "Well…"

"Well, nothing. If you want me back, you need to get me to feel what I *felt* for you before you fucking ripped my heart out." I stood up and took a long draw from my ice-cold pint. "It was *you* who called *me* and wanted me back. I have a life that exists outside your little world," I drew an imaginary circle with my hand that held the beer… encompassing the crew, who were all carousing just beyond where she stood. "Excuse me." I stood and skirted past her without another look.

Once outside, I took a seat in one of the posh blue lounges that were arranged in small groups just beyond the bar, and dialed work.

"Keflavik base security main office, Petty Officer Starr."

"Hi, Jude. It's Garren. Is Archibladt around?"

"Dirk has back-gate duty. I'll patch you through now."

"Thanks." The phone clicked, then went silent. I was beginning to wonder if I'd been disconnected, when the line crackled to life.

"Security, NAS Keflavik rcar-gate, Petty Officer Archibladt." The phone line crackled.

"Jeezus, Dirk, what did you do to get back-gate security detail?" I laughed.

"HOLY FUCK, Noah! What are you doing calling me? I figured by now, you'd be balls deep in Vi," he laughed good-naturedly.

"Been there. Done that," I chuckled and took a slug off my beer. "So, what did you do to get the junk duty detail?"

"Well, without you here to cover my ass by getting me to work on time, I overslept after a long night with Sammie."

"Oh? What happened—was it just the two of you or…?" I couldn't disguise the curiosity in my voice.

"If you're asking if Tess was along, she wasn't. After the trip she went on with Ari yesterday, she got home, and I guess from what Sam said… she pretty much slept until like 1700 today. Sam woke her up and then, she said that she and Ari had some sort of lover's spat."

"What the fuck? What do you mean they had a lover's spat?" I was furious. *I've only been gone a day and a half and here she is already hooking up with Ari! I knew I couldn't trust him around her. And her! What the fuck?!*

"Cool your heels, soldier, it's not like the hooked up or anything. Sam said she could hear the two of them fighting before dinner, all the way from the kitchen."

I interrupted, "So, what did she say it was about?"

"Why the Tessa interrogation? Shouldn't you be worrying about Vi and Suri?"

"Whatever, and I haven't even met Suri yet. So, what did she say happened?"

"You haven't met Suri yet?"

"No. She's with the nanny since Vi's been on a photo shoot all day. She didn't think this party yacht we're on was the place for a kid, I guess. So, what did Tess and Ari have to fight about?"

"It sounded like—and this is *only* from Sammie, so it doesn't make it one hundred percent factual—but I guess he was bent that she's still hooked on you because you don't deserve her. At least, according to Ari. He tried to kiss her after professing how much he liked her."

"*FUCKER!*" I growled the explicative under my breath. "I knew he couldn't be trusted."

"Yeah, well… she can be, cause she shot him down. Hard."

"Good for her!"

"Yeah, well he isn't the only one…"

"What do you mean, he isn't the only one?"

"Sam also mentioned that Tessa shared that her division officer tried to get chummy on their sight-seeing trip yesterday."

"No shit." I shook my head and pounded the last of my beer. "She shot him down, right?"

"She misses you, man. Even if she hadn't, you couldn't blame her for trying to move on after you dumped her for Vi."

I drew in a deep breath, and it hissed out of me like I was gut punched. "Is she…" ahem. I cleared away a strange, tightening in my throat. "I mean, is she trying to move on already?"

"Shit, Noah, I'm not sure, but… could you blame her? I told you she was in a bad way right after you left. Sammie told me she slept for nearly eighteen hours—from the time she went to bed yesterday until she woke up for dinner today."

"Another beer, sir?"

I looked at the younger staff member who had brought me the phone and pointed to the empty pint that I'd set on the table. "The stout."

"Which one, the Guinness, Nut Brown…?"

I interrupted him, "Genevieve will know. The same one, please." I looked at him, "Oh, and thank you."

He nodded and left me to my conversation with Dirk.

"She hasn't left yet, for Turkey I mean?"

"Not until tomorrow. Oh, and, you should know that she and Ari made up pretty much right after their spat, but you can't blame her for that either. I mean, she does have to work with him for the next week, or however long their det. is."

"I know. It just really sucks, especially since things aren't going… Well, they aren't going the way I'd planned them to." I placed my elbows on my knees and my head in my hands, holding the large satellite phone to my ear with my shoulder.

"Sorry, man. That sucks."

"You have no idea." I sighed heavily. I was uncomfortable even talking about this shit, but it was weighing on me heavily, and who the fuck else was I going to talk to? "Have a sec?"

He laughed. "Yeah. It's not exactly like the cars are lining up to come through this gate. What's up?"

I shrugged just as the young, blonde crew member brought me my new pint. I accepted it and mouthed, "Thanks." Bringing the ice-cold stout to my mouth, I took a long, hard hit from it. "Ahhh. Now, that's some good beer."

"Sure, rub it in. You know we have to be dry before and on duty."

"Sorry, man."

"So, what did you want to ask me?" Dirk said something to the security guy he was on duty with and I heard the shack door open and close.

"A car at the gate?"

"You know it. Kelly is checking their sticker and ID. So, are you going to tell me what's up with you and Vi? I mean, I am assuming that's what you wanted to talk about?"

"I don't know. It's just… well, nothing is going like I'd planned."

I could hear him say something to Kelly, so I paused for them to finish.

"Everything with Vi's weird now."

"Maybe it isn't her? I mean, Noah, you've been in a pretty intense relationship up here. Maybe Tess meant more to you than you knew?"

"Yeah, maybe. I mean, I knew my feelings for Tessa were complicated, but I think maybe you're right… it's just," I sighed—searching for the right words. "I just kinda thought I'd show up and the love I felt for Vi would still be there but turns out I'm pretty pissed off. I mean, sometimes I look at her and am so mad I want to punch her in the face—not that I ever would—but you know what I mean?"

"Yeah, I've been there a few times myself, with one of my exes in particular… I was afraid if we stayed together, I'd do something I'd regret."

"Well, when it happened to you, were you ever confused? Cause as much as I want to hit her sometimes, other times, I look at her and just want to fuck her brains out. I'm so goddamn mixed up, and now she's got me on this damn luxury yacht—"

Dirk interrupted me, "Luxury yacht!? Fuck, Noah! Life must be really rough," he quipped sarcastically.

"It's like a goddamn prison. She's around every corner, and we're running so hot and cold, I don't know what to expect of her. I mean, one minute I'm sunbathing, and she jumps my bones, so everyone leaves us to fuck. The next, she's jealous cause I'm flirting with the bartender and we're fighting. This roller coaster is making me so damn sick, I don't know which way's up, and which is down." *And, I haven't even been able to meet my daughter yet!* I lamented to myself.

"No shit? Wow, sorry your leave is suckin' so bad."

"Yeah, tell me about it."

"Why has she kept you from Suri? I mean, don't you think it's a little weird?"

I leaned back in my lounge and filled my mouth with another quenching pull from my stout. "Yeah. I mean no? Fuck, I don't know. She met me at the pier when I got in this morning wearing a skimpy bikini and sarong. She said she'd had a shoot at sunrise and had left Suri with the nanny. We had breakfast and then headed back to her hotel we both needed a shower, her to remove the salt water, and me the travel grime...

well, we practically fucked, but she'd played the coy temptress and held off.

Shortly after, we boarded the yacht her agent or somebody had booked for the shoot she's on now. I mean, I think Pallavi should've made my meeting Suri a priority, but at the same time, I knew when I came here that she had to work… so it also makes sense that she'd keep our daughter out of this environment. I guess, after we get back tomorrow, I'll get to meet her? She hasn't said exactly when—she hasn't said yet whether she's working tomorrow —but that's my assumption…."

"I mean, from what you're telling me it doesn't sound ideal, but it doesn't sound as bad as you made it out to be either."

"Dirk, it's *so* fucked. I thought I'd see her, and all these emotions would come flooding back into my head. I thought when we fucked, that it would be—and I know this will sound cheesy as all hell—but I thought I'd feel more, and we'd be making love like how it was years ago."

"Yeah, but a lot has happened since then. You guys aren't the same people."

"Mostly, I had no idea Tessa would be haunting me like she is. I thought when my dick was in Vi, that I'd have her on my mind… but instead Tessa…" My voice cracked when I said her name, and I swallowed heavily, trying to figure out my feelings, what I wanted to share, fuck, what advice I was asking for, but came up with nothing. "Tessa's raspberry lips, her perfect tits and to die for abs, fuck… her ass and legs," I cleared my throat. "Jeezus, Dirk, she has a platinum grade pussy…" I laughed uncomfortably. "You just have no idea how amazing she is. And, I mean with *everything* she does. It's actually pretty remarkable."

Dirk also chuckled uneasily, "TMI, dude! Nah, just joking, but seriously… Tess isn't as great as all that."

"Oh, no? What makes you say that?" I was curious as hell where he'd the idea that she wasn't.

"I'd be willing to bet that at one point you'd thought Vi was as amazing as Tessa, right?"

"Well, yeah, sure. Why?"

"Well, I'm no love doctor, and you know I don't know shit when it comes to women—I mean, look at the crap affair I'm in with Sam—but I do know this: when I've been in love with someone, they're the best fucking lay, the best dick-sucker, the best cook… you name it. You thought Vi was the best when you loved her, but she seems to have been replaced now that you love Tessa."

BOOM! There it is. In my face. He just heaved a big ol' pile of shit at my feet. Why did I think I could end things with Tessa and move easily back into a relationship with Vi? I'm fucking stupid.

"I'm so torn, man! I feel like I should keep trying to get this thing with Vi back on track since we have Suri together, but it isn't happening organically, and I'm just not sure what to do anymore. I feel like I'm a bad guy if I don't try to make us a family."

"Hey, I'm total shit when it comes to good advice. I'm telling you this again because that's exactly what this next advice is—shit. But, maybe, you just need to get loaded on booze and whatever else, fuck Vi silly, have her suck your dick—a lot—and put Tessa out of your mind until your dick makes the decision for you. You know the saying, "Love the one your with?""

I laughed half-heartedly. "Dirk, your advice sucks green donkey dick." I laughed and finished off the last of my pint. "Well, thanks for the Tessa update. Hey, you never did say why you were assigned the rear-gate detail. What did you and Sam do all night that kept you out so late you missed muster?"

"Oh, Noah," he said warily, as though he were reliving it, "we grabbed a ride with some of her friends and went to the natural hot springs not far from Keflavik. We dropped acid and then roasted ourselves in the springs while we zoned to the Northern Lights. We fucked like bunnies and then kinda passed out until I woke up hurling. We didn't make it onto base until early morning—like 0400 or so. I crashed in their room and when Sam came to, it was 1030ish. I was four hours late, so I got Rothleer's duty, since he's light-duty for a week."

"Oh, man! That sucks! What happened to Rothleer?"

"He was in a fender-bender in the Commissary parking lot. They said he suffered from a mild whiplash and was put on light duty for a week. Eight workdays. Now I have his detail until he's cleared for regular duty."

"Shit, and I thought my life sucked." I roared with laughter. Dirk joined me, and by the time we caught our breaths, I was feeling more relaxed and clear-headed. "Thanks, man, but I'd better get back to making a go of this with Pallavi."

"Anytime. I mean, I know my advice sucks, but, I'm here if you need me. You're my brother."

"Thanks, man." We said our goodbyes and hung up.

My timing couldn't have been any, better because no sooner had I set the phone down, then Pallavi rounded the lounge I was sprawled out on and asked if she could join me.

"Sure, sexy, I'd like that."

"Does this mean you forgive me? I didn't mean to get jealous, it's just I can't stand how women throw themselves at you. I mean, I know you're a nice guy, and so you flirt as a way to let them down easily. You'd never entertain hooking up with her since you're with me. It's just hard, you know?"

I pulled her into me, wrapping my arm around her shoulders. "Sorry if I was being insensitive. This whole trip just has so much riding on it, it frankly has me on edge." I leaned down and kissed the tip of her cute little nose. She snuggled deeper into the crook under my arm.

"Turns out lunch is running late, and after talking to Antonine, he's decided to put off getting more frames in until after the crew comes down some off their boozy high."

I chuckled, "So, this means we have just 'us' time?"

"That's exactly what it means." she stretched her neck and her lips met mine in a modest, apprehensive kiss that said she was as unsure as I was about us.

"Well," I said, smiling easily at her, "I'm all yours. What would you like to do?"

"I spoke with Antonine and the captain before heading out here to find you; they're pulling us into a quiet cove on the far side of the island where the waters are shallow, the waves are calm, and the sands are warm. When they mentioned it, it sounded like the perfect spot for us to unwind and get to know one another with no pressure."

"I couldn't agree more." I reached for her head, guiding it towards mine, where my lips met hers in an unhurried, relaxed and stress-free kiss. Our lips moved in sync and hers parted at the slightest pressure. I pulled her to my chest. Her hard nipples teased my skin and brought goosebumps to the surface. I deepened our kiss, drawing her tongue into my mouth, exploring hers, which elicited a sexy moan from deep in the back of her throat. I broke the kiss short when I felt my dick start to get hard. I didn't want the pressure he'd add to the situation.

"How long until we get there?"

"The cove? I don't know, but probably less than an hour."

"Why don't we head up to the top deck, share a chaise lounge and take a quick nap?"

"Oh, baby, that's right—you probably haven't slept well since before you left on Friday huh?"

"Actually, I partied with Dirk all night, so the last time I slept was Thursday, I mean, not counting the catnaps I got in on the plane." I pulled her up with me as I stood, wrapping my arm around her slim waist, and led her towards what I hoped would be a peaceful respite.

Tina Maurine

-FIVE-

We'd been awakened by the 'surfer' crew member—River, as he'd finally introduced himself. I figured his name would be easily remembered, as he resembled the late River Phoenix.

Pallavi and I had done a couple rounds of shots and then made our way down to the swim deck off the stern. She'd slipped comfortably into her birthday suit—*Jeezus! Fuck, she has a rockin' body!*—t hen sauntered over to me and wrapped her svelte arms around my waist.

"I will never grow tired of touching you." She ran her fingers over my back. My muscles tensed and flexed as they made their way from my shoulder blades to my waist. "Your skin against my fingertips does things to me—see? Look!" She pulled back far enough to show me how tight her nipple buds had become.

"Impressive."

I smirked arrogantly and opened my mouth to say more, but she interrupted me. "If you need more proof," she ground her intimates into mine, "all you have to do is reach down here and see what you do to me."

I smacked her ass and hoisted her up over my shoulder.

"Oh no you don't," she squealed delightedly.

I smacked her ass again playfully and slid her down from her perch on my shoulder, down across my abdomen until I was able to cradle carry her, cupping her behind her back and under her knees.

"Hold your breath," I grated out huskily and jumped, holding her while plunged into the calm ocean. We surfaced and swam toward shore, maybe twenty feet before we could stand.

"Hey, what's that?" I motioned toward the boat, then splashed her with water.

"YOU! I'm gonna get you!" She lunged after me, but it appeared as though she moved in slow motion. I quickly dove out of the way. We frolicked playfully for a few minutes until I let her catch me. She dunked me, but when I surfaced, she greeted me, wrapping her arms around my neck and her long, slender legs around my waist. The water was tepid, but her bare skin against mine ignited a fire in me, heating me at my core.

"Mmm, isn't this nice?" she purred below my ear, her lips grazing my neck.

"Yeah, it's exactly what we needed." I squeezed her tightly and strode, with her wrapped around me, to shore. She teased me all the while, squeezing me with her bare thighs and running kisses delicately from my collarbone to my ear, her fingers interwoven in my hair. Once we reached the beach, I lowered her to the sand. Her full breasts slid across my abdomen, causing my traitorous dick to twitch again. *Bastard!*

I loved that Pallavi, although the vision of dainty and proper fell short on all counts but one… she ate like a mouse. Otherwise, she cussed like a sailor, guzzled beer, could hold her shots, and, hell, pretty much dove in feet first with whatever scenario I gave her—like now. Here she was butt-ass naked and already sitting in the sand.

"You planning on joining me any time soon?" She was leaning back on her elbows, tits up, tan legs extended, long black hair grazing the dry sand. *What a beauty. No wonder she was discovered as soon as she set foot in the US…*

I strode the short distance to the smooth sand she'd found and lowered myself down beside her. "Can you blame me for enjoying the scenery?" I cocked my brow and smirked arrogantly, my gaze drawn back down to her perfect, firm tits. It blew my mind that her body looked this amazing after having our daughter. How many women would die to look this good, even before they'd had kids?

The sand was warm and inviting, and I laid back, hands behind my head, and closed my eyes.

"Can I ask you something?"

I turned my head towards her, cracking my eyelid open and peeking from under it at her. She was scrutinizing me intently. I watched her as her eyes traveled from my head, across my muscular physique, settling momentarily on the impressive bulge I still had in my pants, before bringing her gaze back up to my face. I reclosed my eyes.

"Noah, baby?"

"Hmm?"

"I've been wondering. I mean, it's been so long since we've talked, and I wondered if you've been single all this time."

There's no way I was going to make this easy for her. "All *what* time?"

"You know." She paused uncomfortably.

Curiosity got the better of me, and I rolled over and opened my eyes, finding her honey-brown ones. We held each other's gaze for the briefest moment, before I smiled and rolled back over onto my back.

"So, there's been something that's been killing me for a long time now."

"Oh?"

"Why did you leave that morning?"

What the fuck? What does she mean why did I leave? "Can we not do this?"

"I think it is important, Ya Habibi. I feel we need to get past these old feelings in order to move forward with a newer, stronger us." She hesitated. "So, I've always wondered why you left that morning when you saw Ahmed?"

"Fuck, Vi," sarcasm dripped from my tone, "what else should I have done? Given him my bagel and coffee? Had a seat on the bed beside you and shared yours? Give me a fucking break." I rolled onto my stomach and faced away from her.

"He was there because he'd found me, but not because he'd planned to take me home. Hell, at that point, Ahmed hadn't even made a plan what he'd do once he saw me. He literally had just walked in the door when your lift arrived."

"I saw him there in a puddle of water. You guys were arguing." I rolled back to face her, my eyes connected with her pained ones. "I saw him standing there. You were on the bed, crying hysterically, rocking yourself… I mean, what should I've done?"

"You ran away from me instead of to me. I needed you. The month we had together was sublime. It really meant something to me, you know?"

"Yeah. I *DO* know. You were *it* for me, Vi. The two years we wrote letters back and forth covertly finally seemed worth it when you called me from New York. When I was with you that month, I didn't need my therapy sessions, my breathing treatments. I didn't need anything but you. I'd thought I'd found my future in you… obviously not." I shrugged dismally. .

"Why didn't you even call me? I mean, Noah, you completely dropped off the grid."

"Well, I didn't—and still don't—know what happened between you and your husband. What's his name again?"

"Ahmed."

"Right. Ahmed. I figured he was your husband and he'd come from Kuwait to fetch you." I faltered. *What I wouldn't do for a fucking beer right about now.* "I didn't call because you were having an affair with me, and we both know how bad it can be for women in your culture when you're caught with another man. Especially since you were married to a traditional man, which I had no way of knowing, since you'd never spoken of him. Why didn't you tell me you were married in at least one of the secret letters you wrote me during those two years? During one of our stolen moments while I was there? All you ever said was your family wouldn't approve of you marrying an American, not 'hey, Noah I'm already married.' FUCK, Vi!" It was all I could do to keep my composure, if anyone could call it that. "You ask me why I didn't call. Are you fucking serious?"

"Our parents are traditional, and it was an arranged marriage. He'd actually come to figure out a way for us to both get out of it, but we ended up getting along better in New York than we'd ever had back home. There was too much pressure from both sides of our families for kids, the perfect job, blah, blah, blah. In New York, we were both just kids from Kuwait."

"Then why would you have wanted me to call, Vi? Sounds like the two of you were meant for each other."

"He and I only happened because you jumped ship."

"Whatever. You're not taking any responsibility in this. You called me the first time I was in Havelock, North Carolina. It's not like you couldn't have called again. *You* had *my* number, Vi. It was *you* who never called." I sat up and drew my knees to my chest, wrapping my arms loosely around them. I looked back at her as she lay there bronzed, naked, and emotionally bare. "Listen, Vi," I sighed deeply, "this isn't getting us anywhere. I came this week when you called because you said it was over with him, and you wanted to give it a try with me again. You wanted me to meet our daughter and try to be a family, the way it should've been."

"I know. Sorry to have sprung it on you, Ya Habibi, the way I did, but I've felt it was over with Ahmed for a long time now, plus ana bahebak."

"Do you?" I shook my head in disbelief, wanting it to be true. *But why did it take her so long to call me?* "Do you love me? I mean, I know you once did six years ago… but how do you know it's still how you feel? I'm not the same person. Neither of us is."

"I know, but that's why I wanted you here. It is a beautiful, romantic location, and I figured, what better place to fall back in love?" She reached out and placed her long fingers on my calf.

"You ripped my heart out. I was alone, searching for some sort of fulfillment for so long, fucking my way through women and just hoping one of them would make me feel something for them like you had."

"Oh, Noah, I'm so…"

I cut her off, "It took me years—*years*—to find someone who touched my heart… and then I lost *her* before I even had her." I rested my forehead on my crossed arms, closing my eyes and letting Tessa, of her beautiful, strong features and memories of the first time we'd met at her going away party, flood into my mind. My heart swelled in a way that was different than when I thought of Pallavi. *How can I love them both, but so differently?* I shook my head, trying to make sense of the madness.

"Then, she literally danced back into my life the night before I got the call that you and Ahmed were over. She and I had just met, and although I wasn't entirely sure it was her, I was drawn to this woman like a fucking moth to a flame. She was dangerous for me, but in all the right ways." I looked up and saw Pallavi's shoulders slump heavily as she swiped at her cheek with the back of her hand.

"Who is she?"

"Tessa Christy," I said her name almost reverently. *Fuck, I missed her so much.* Again, I wondered what kind of irreparable damage I'd done by coming here. *I still have to see Suri, so I can't bag on this just yet. Suri needs me as her dad. It's my right to raise my own kid.*

"So, you're still with her, then?" her voice piped in a quivery tone. "Like, with her with her?"

"Actually, no. She and I ended it when I decided to see if you and I still had anything."

"Wow. She let you go that easily? I'd say she isn't the one for you at all."

"Well, *Vi*, you *don't* have a fucking say in the matter. She didn't let me go. I decided to come here, and she decided she didn't want to be my second choice." I cleared my throat. "I wouldn't have expected any less from her." My tone grew soft. "She's an amazing woman."

"She must be to have you turned this inside out."

I just nodded.

Tina Maurine

-SIX-

It wasn't long before the yacht's skiff arrived on the gleaming white beach. Antonine and his crew stepped onto the powdery sand, and the hurricane they brought with them swept away the small morsel of tranquility Pallavi and I had found after our earlier discussion. They began setting up back-lights and had pulled her off the sand, having her try on a few different patches of fabric. I couldn't really call them swimsuits since they wouldn't have functioned in the water—*at all*. River and Genevieve worked at fashioning a picnic of sorts, removing plastic wrap from meat and cheese trays. I glanced over. and it appeared they'd some veggies and fruits too. *GOOD, I'm so damn hungry I could eat a horse.* Genevieve saw me eyeing the food ravenously.

"Could I fix you a plate, sir?" Her soft timbre surprised me, but not as much as the tunes the crew had just cranked up. Addled, I turned to see what was going on, and unexpectedly, Pallavi captivated me. She took center stage, provocatively dancing to Usher's "You Make Me Wanna," while her photographer Omar snapped shots. The sun was dropping, now not far from the horizon, and the rich burnt oranges and burgundies ricocheted off every surface. Pallavi looked on fire; her skin glowed like smoldering embers and her hair flashed as its shine reflected all the colors of the sunset. I was mesmerized by her goddess-like appearance.

Startled, I accepted the 4oz whiskey rock glass that River handed to me. He silently toasted me, raising his beer up and settling back against the palm that I'd taken refuge against. We stared, jaws agape. Pallavi moved, *nay*—she flowed—from one pose to the next. She flirted with the camera, and I guarantee the guys who saw her in *Maxim* or whatever magazine she was shooting for would archive this copy in their spank library.

"Daaamn!"

I looked over at River, but I doubt he even noticed he'd said anything. "She's something else, isn't she?" I raised my glass in her direction.

"Where's she from," his question fell softly from his mouth in awed wonder.

"I met her when I was stationed in Kuwait nearly six years ago."

He looked at me, obvious shock etched on his face. "Well, I'm going there to find me a wife."

I laughed at the earnest belief in his declaration.

"No, seriously. Look at her, man! And those eyes—are those real or made-up? You know, with make-up and stuff?"

I chuckled at his blatant fascination with Pallavi. "Nope, no make-up on her eyes. She's never needed it." Pallavi's eyes were outlined in thick, uncommon double rows of dark eyelashes that made her eyes look like she wore eyeliner all the time, when in fact, she never needed it. He was right; it was one of her best features—not that any of them were lacking. "How about this?" River looked at me, "If it doesn't work out with us, you can give it a try."

"Huh?"

"Vi and I are dating…"

"Shut the fuck up! Whoa, dude!"

I continued where I left off before he interrupted me. "We're dating, and if it doesn't work out, then I'm telling you right now that you have the green light to ask her out."

"Shoot—I'd love to, but I'd lose my job. Trust me, this kind of gig is not the kind that you want to lose… Dolla', dolla' bills, YO!" We laughed and resumed our admiration of Pallavi.

Vexed

After a few more suits and songs, the crew broke for the grub Genevieve had laid out. It was meant to be a quick snack, and not even five minutes into it, Pallavi approached me.

"Ana bahebak, Ya Habibi." She molded into my body, hugging me tightly. "Antonine said he knows of a great locale a short walk inland—there's falls and a stream." She squealed delightedly, "When we get back, which will be soon, cause there's so little light, we can… you know?" She stood up on her toes and drew my bottom lip into her mouth, then kissed them both seductively. I nodded and smacked her on her ass as she turned.

After she'd left, I'd made myself useful by helping River and Genevieve pack up and load the remaining food, coolers, trash, and service—both clean and the ones we'd used—onto the skiff. The photography crew had packed in very little from the beach, with them into the jungle-like foliage so we'd broken down all of the lighting umbrellas and the case full of Pallavi's wardrobe. We picked up some beer bottle caps and loose trash that had made their way down the beach. Honestly, I didn't think the light would be good enough for any photos, so I was surprised to hear, when they bounced out of the lush vegetation, that they'd gotten some 'keepers.'

"Noah, right?" Omar came up beside me and showed me some frames of Pallavi he'd gotten on his digital camera. "She's a masterpiece, isn't she?" He looked at her and she glowed at his compliment. "It's so refreshing to work with someone who knows what they're doing for a change. There's so much new blood nowadays, that it's a vacation when I get to work with veterans in this industry."

I was still looking through the frames that he'd captured. "Omar, you're amazing, man. These are…"

He interrupted me and pulled gently on the camera strap until I relinquished his equipment. "It's not me, I'm just the tool that captures her beauty." Omar shot me daggers. *What the fuck? That's right, keep on walking, fucker!*

"Don't mind him." The wardrobe gal had seen the whole thing. "Hi, I'm Kate."

I looked at her over my shoulder. "Hey."

"I see this a lot, especially with the veteran photographers. In this industry, a good photo is *NEVER* because of a talented photographer or crew. The credit always goes to the model. I'm sure he didn't mean anything by it, but he's good at what he does, and that's just one of the reasons he's in such high demand."

I turned and saw a modest gal with curly red hair, of average build and height. She was cute enough, and images of Tessa, with her beautiful red tendrils, popped into my mind. We were so far away from each other—half a world away— and emotionally in separate universes, but she was never far from my thoughts. *My sweet Tessa.* I missed her, everything about her, even the nuances that had driven me crazy before.

The wind was picking up; it looked like maybe a storm was blowing in. Everyone had finished checking the beach for items left behind, so we all piled into the skiff for a choppy ride back to the yacht, which was now lit up like New Years. Strings of white lights hung in rows from the center cabins to both the bow and stern. It was pretty fucking awesome, I have to admit, and I couldn't believe it was where I was staying for the night.

We disembarked and spread out to our own cabins. I headed off in the direction the guys from the photography crew headed.

"Noah! Hey, Noah, wait!" I turned and saw Pallavi running after me, her arm was crossed over her chest to keep from bouncing around. "Where are you off to?"

"My room, I guess."

"You're in the master suite with me."

Duh. I guess that makes sense. "Well, I hadn't heard and didn't want to assume…"

"Don't be silly. Shoot… seeing if we're compatible is the reason you came all this way." I nodded. "Besides, I had your backpack stowed in there when we boarded."

"Well, guess that means I'm definitely going with you, cause I have got to get the sand out of my crack," I joked. "It's killing me."

We headed to the master suite by way of a dark wood staircase that wound its way up to the second deck. We entered into a well-appointed living/entertaining space with several groupings of plush chairs around low tables. There was a liquor bar here just like the lounge on the sun-deck we'd been at earlier in the day. The furniture was all high-end leather and decorated in black and white; faux furs accented the floor and pops of black and red adorned the furniture. It was tastefully decorated in an eclectic mix of modern and nautical styles that somehow worked.

"We're right through here," she said, grabbing my hand and leading me through the back of the lounge, past the bar and bathrooms and down a hallway, to the impressive double doors at the end. She paused, turned and leaned into me, pulling my head down to meet her lips in a wild kiss that spoke volumes. She settled back onto her heels on the floor in front of me, still looking into my eyes. Confusion washed over my face. "Please give me tonight. Give yourself to me, Ya Habibi, free from judgment, so we can make us right again."

I raised an eyebrow, as skeptical as I was curious about what tonight would bring. "We have a lot to discuss, Vi." I sighed heavily. "Our future needs to bring more to the table than my present in Iceland does. You'll truly *never* know the cost I paid to give this a try with you."

She stood on her toes again, grazing my lips with hers. "I understand, my sweet habibi. I understand." She lowered her hands to the knobs behind her back and turned them as she pushed, backing them open. The doors swung wide. Moonlight shone through the windows, casting incandescent light across the room. Shadows hid in the corners where the magic couldn't reach. A California King sat prominently in the center of the room, drenched in satin and furs. At the head of the bed was a mountain of pillows that would've made my brothers overseas jealous.

Memories of my time in Afghanistan flooded into my head; the Afghan nomads called the Kuchis who we'd run across many times while on patrols or special op. missions in Kabul, as they drove their 600-strong flocks of sheep and goats. They'd been a welcoming people and had invited us into their goat's-wool tarped kegdeies, where we'd lounged on their mountains of furs, pillows and wool blankets, ate mutton from the sheep they'd butchered on our behalf, and shot the shit in Farsi over rancid goat milk.

"Noah? Come back to me, my poor habibi. You're still having flashbacks?" Pallavi molded herself against my back, kissing my shoulder, her concern evident in her attentive actions.

"Rarely, but sometimes." I reached up, taking her hand and gently pulling her in front of me. I nestled my cock against her ass, wrapped my arms around her chest, and nuzzled my face against her neck. Her scent was intoxicating; a sweet rose, chai, nutmeg and vanilla concoction, topped off with almost a hint of maple. "I've always loved the way you smell."

She moaned slightly as she rubbed her firm ass against my growing arousal. "Let's slide open the wall and enjoy each other in the water," she suggested provocatively.

In front of us was a wall of floor to ceiling window panels that could be slid open to make a large indoor-outdoor space. Centered smack dab in the middle of the wall was a party-sized bathtub jacuzzi. Pallavi walked to the windows, flipped open a lock, and easily slid them open to one side. She raised an eyebrow as she traipsed back over to me, gliding her hand down my chest before turning to face the moon's reflection on the ocean, just past the deck of the yacht.

Pallavi slipped her see-through cover-up off her shoulders and shimmied salaciously to get the sheer fabric over her hips… all while standing in front of me, her ass still pressing determinedly against my now hard cock.

"Jeezus, Vi," I grated, panting. My body's response to her was ridiculous. I was like a dog in the proximity of a bitch in heat. My cock throbbed, my heart was speeding, and all I could think about was her long legs around me and her warm pussy welcoming me. End of Story.

She untied the back straps of her bikini top and pulled it over her head, turning to me and pressing her voluptuous chest into my solid one. "Come, undress. Join me." Pallavi reached up, wrapping her arms around my neck as she stood on her toes. Her soft lips grazed mine, and she nipped flirtatiously at my bottom lip before releasing it. Her long fingers went to work stripping me out of my t-shirt, then ripped open the Velcro fly on my board shorts. As the fabric dropped off my hips and fell to the floor, I pulled the strings of her bikini bottom; the final piece of material that stood between us. It fluttered to the floor and lay next to mine.

She took my hand. I felt like a schoolboy ready to lose his virginity, I was so excited. *How many times have I wanted this, dreamt she'd want me like this again?* I followed her eagerly and was surprised to see that the tub had been filled for us already. Rose oil, from the smell of it, and milk bath-beads had been added to the water. She threw her million-dollar legs over the side and slid in. I followed, not in the least bit conscious about how absurd I probably looked. Sure, I was naked, but there was no one's skin I'd rather be in. I knew I looked decent, and, well, fuck. My cock was hard and big enough—at least I'd *never* had a complaint—only call-backs. I smiled to myself.

"Feeling pretty arrogant, are you?" I heard the teasing lilt in her voice.

"Don't confuse arrogance with confidence," I stated playfully.

Once in the water, I pulled her onto my lap, splaying her legs, one on either side of my thighs. I supported Pallavi's full weight—all 105lbs of her, dripping wet. The water between her breasts and my bare chest was heated, but not as warm as the water between her bare pussy and my erection. "You need to stop wiggling, or you're going to start something I won't want to stop," I growled huskily, tracing my rough hands down her back and along the full sides of her breasts.

"Maybe," she lured challengingly, "I *want* you to start something." She reached down to where my hard dick rested firmly against my abdomen. "Tell me, Noah, do you like it when I do this?" It took both of her slender hands to hold my shaft, causing my sharp, immediate intake of breath. When she squeezed, my whole body jerked, my head lolling back.

"God, woman." I cleared my throat, the passion heavy in my tone. I gasped sharply at the feelings she was evoking below the veil of water. "If you're teasing me, you need to stop." I tried to be as stern as possible, but she took no heed.

"Or," and she paused again seductively, "how about when I do this?" She positioned the head of my cock at her entrance, and sharply slid down on me, sheathing me fully. "How's this?" she cooed. "Do you like it when I do this?" She placed her feet flat on the Jacuzzi floor and used her thigh muscles to jounce and gyrate on my hard dick.

I clenched my teeth, clinging onto restraint, the vision of Pallavi riding my heavy cock, her tits flouncing in the water. The sexy flush spreading across her cheeks, with her head back and her neck elongated—*fuck me*—it nearly sent me over the edge. My lips met hers with a feverishness that I'd only felt with…

Tessa…

I drove my hands into her long tresses, imprisoning her, commandeering the kiss. I took it from flirty-passionate to an undeniably tempestuous passion. Pallavi was no longer in control, and I stole every ounce of desire from her that I could usurp. My mouth pillaged and plundered hers, robbing her breath from her lips before she could drag in a replenishing intake of breath. My tongue scourged hers, tormenting her lips with brutal passion.

"Don't slow down," I grated. "Harder. Faster." I could feel her pussy clenching around my engorged erection; she was close. I needed more from her, so I pulled my hands from her locks and plunged them into the water, anchoring them on her hip bones. "Straddle me," I commanded. "Sit down completely—I need you deeper." My words snarled from between clenched teeth, every muscle in my body straining for my imminent release.

She obeyed me, and when I felt her pussy flush with the root of my shaft, and her ass sitting heavily on my nuts, I began rocking her hips feverishly forward and back as I pistoned my cock, driving deeply into her with each thrust.

Her hands grasped and clawed at my shoulders, fighting frantically for some measure of control, but I was unrelenting in my deliverance, determined for her to get hers before I took mine. I took her assailed appearance in; her lose hair that clung to her neck and shoulders, her red and swollen breasts…

"Noah… Oh my… God! NOAH!"

My eyes flew up to hers, saw them stormy and hooded with passion. I continued my assault on her, rocking her on my cock, drilling into her with each forward tilt. Her hands flew up to my face, cupping my cheeks in her palms. Her mahogany eyes bored into mine, unwavering.

"Yes... YES… Oh my, *fuck*. YES!" Pallavi broke. She shattered into a million pieces before me, her body raked with spasmodic waves. I thrust deeply a final time, pouring my load into her, pulse after throbbing pulse. My chest tightened, and I found it impossible to take in the air I needed. She crumpled onto me as I struggled to regain my composure. I lifted her off of me. I needed to breathe. I needed space, space away from… *her*.

My mind filled with images from the past couple of months in Iceland—*fuck me*—not the images I should've been conjuring up. I leaned over, grazed Pallavi's forehead with the obligatory kiss and climbed quickly out of the tub. I grabbed a folded towel, wrapped it tightly around my waist and stepped outside onto the deck, into the dark, welcoming the cool breeze.

Images of Tessa continued to flood into my mind. *What the fuck's wrong with me?* I thought. I'd just fucked Pallavi, something I'd wanted to do since this afternoon's session. In fact, it was something I'd dreamt of doing since walking out of her flat all those years ago. My orgasm had been mind-shattering. She'd felt every bit as amazing as I'd imagined she would, in spite of knowing she'd been plowed regularly, and by who knows how many men. It amazed me how little I cared.

What I did care about, though, was how I envisioned Tessa would react if, *when,* I told her. How hurt and betrayed she'd feel. *We're broken up, so why the guilt?* Why the fuck was I feeling so terrible after just blowing my goddamn load?

"Noah?"

I turned to face the shadow-lit suite. Pallavi was hard to make out, except for her towel, which shone brightly, as though lit up by black lights. I stood there staring at her. Eventually, with nothing to say, I turned back to the ocean, my mind ravaged and torn. I thought about her *and* Tessa. The two of them were tearing me apart. I'd had no idea this trip would cause the pain I was feeling over losing Tessa and the poignant lack of joy over Pallavi. I had expected to rejoice in our reunion and feel love—new and old. Instead, I felt only confusion, with a side of regret.

"Noah?" Pallavi cozied up next to me from behind, hugging me around my waist. "See, wasn't that what we needed?" she purred it, oblivious to how I felt, which greatly perplexed me. She and I had been so on point when I'd met her in the Middle East, and when we'd spent that month together in New York. Hell, if it hadn't been for her husband—who I'd been made to understand had been out of the picture—arriving that day, I'd always believed we'd still be together. Now, I wasn't so sure. We'd lost *IT*, whatever it was, and I'd found a new *IT* with Tessa, and thrown it away for… *THIS*. I shook my head, frustrated at my situation and angry at my choices.

"I knew it would be this way, like no time has passed."

Could she possibly be this dense? I shrugged, "It was definitely sobering." I unclasped her hands, which were imprisoning me, stifling me. "I need some air."

"Ya Habibi," she whined in her baby voice, one that was meant to be sexy, but instead grated on my nerves, "you're already outside. Why don't we draw the furs and pillows from the bed and make a love nest out here?"

I looked at her coldly, more dispassionately that I'd meant to. "No. I mean, I need *air*." I brushed past her, walking beyond the Jacuzzi and dropping my towel. I grabbed my shorts and t-shirt, throwing them on before I made it to the door and pulled it shut behind me with a bang.

Suddenly, clarity crashed over me. Of these two women, one sent waves of emotion through me… unrestrained, unbridled and wild, sweeping away filth and pettiness, everything trivial in her path like a tsunami. So, why, I wondered, should I stand at the shores of the other's ocean and waste her time?

I walked to the bar where Omar and Kate, who I'd met earlier, were having a drink. Genevieve had her elbows on the bar and was flirting from behind the counter with River, the deck-hand. Their chemistry was palpable, and I was an easy twenty feet from them. I sauntered over and took my seat next to him.

"Jack and Coke. Make it a double." I laid my $20 tip on the counter appreciatively. Genevieve pocketed it, squeezing River's hand before uprighting herself and going to make my drink.

River looked over. "What's up, man?" he smiled disingenuously. "Rough night?"

"Fuck. You have no idea." I gratefully took the drink placed in front of me and slammed half of it down.

"Well, if there's anything I can do for you, let me know."

I nodded, deadpan, and took another long draw from my stiff drink, swirling the bottom in the cubes of ice. I threw the last sip back and slid my glass toward Genevieve for a refill.

She glanced back over at me, sighed, smiled at River, and stood to go fetch me my poison.

I leaned in, smiling mischievously. "I just left Pallavi, ready and raring to go…"

His eyes widened, then he glanced in the direction Genevieve was behind the bar. "The model who was shooting on the beach today?"

I nodded, "You should go, slugger." I nudged him and winked.

Just then, Genevieve placed my drink in front of me loudly. Her eyes narrowed when I returned her gaze naively.

I looked back at River, hoping maybe if he went and fucked Pallavi's brains out, then I wouldn't have to do any explaining later for my behavior. Unfortunately, all I got was a shrug.

"Hey," I said offhandedly, "you know, there is something you can get for me… have a phone?"

"Local or International?"

"I'm calling Iceland."

He glanced back to Genevieve, who, in her defense, was handling my repeated intrusions like a champ, leaned in and whispered something in her ear before standing. "Noah, right?" I nodded. "Give me a minute, I'll go try to rustle one up for you on the bridge."

"Thanks." I tossed out over my shoulder, picking up my heavy-pour Jack and Coke.

"So, what's your story?" Genevieve eyed me suspiciously. Gone was the friendly gal I'd met earlier when we'd first boarded.

I took a quenching swallow. "What do you mean?" I asked as I swirled the cubes in the half-full whiskey rock glass.

She leaned in. "You know, what's up with you and the supermodel?"

"*Nothing.* My story and its happy ending ended when I got on a plane to come here." I was starting to feel the booze already. The first pour must have been strong as well, and I hadn't had much to eat today. I could feel the heat creeping up my neck and across my forehead.

"So, it's a sad story then," she placed her hand on the back of mine. "Well, I can get you drunk enough you can rewrite the ending or forget it. Either way, the next one's on me."

"It's an open bar, *sweetheart*," sarcasm dripped from my tongue.

"Whatever, it was metaphorical." She rolled her eyes, then glanced up. River was already making a beeline towards me, a cell in his hand.

When he reached me, he offered it and I handed him a twenty for his time. "Where's the satellite phone?"

"The first mate was on it, the captain tossed me his for you to use."

"He doesn't mind that it's to Iceland?"

"Nope. Comes with the rental."

I nodded, picked my drink up, pointed at it to indicate I'd want another, and took it to a plush leather lounger, staged a fair distance from the bar, dialing as I walked.

"Keflavik Base Security, main office, Petty Officer Cordet."

"Hey, Kel, it's Garren."

"Hey, Noah. So you either really miss us, or your leave is suckin'," she joshed cheerfully. "We're understaffed—there's a bad stomach thing going around—so I think Archibladt is pulling a double too. If you wait a sec, I can check the duty schedule."

"Thanks," I offered. I was edgy and just wanted to talk to… *Tessa*… but Dirk would have to do.

The phone crackled. "Yup, sure enough, it looks like he's still at the rear gate. Want me to put ya through?" She lowered her voice. "I'd let it ring until he picks up. It's been a long day, if you get my drift."

"Thanks, Kel."

"Sure thing. Try to go more than a day without worrying about what's going on here. Enjoy your leave okay?"

I laughed maniacally. I was distressed, and the idea of enjoying more time with Pallavi was enough to send me over the edge. "Yeah," I managed, "sure. I'll try."

The phone buzzed and clicked. Then, between crackles, rang and rang. She was right, he must be sleeping.

"Security, NAS Keflavik rear-gate," he yawned mid-sentence, "Petty Officer Archibladt."

"Jeezus, Dirk! Sleeping on the job? It's a good thing I'm not there or I'd have to write you up."

He chuckled, "Hey, Noah! I didn't expect you to be calling so soon. What's up, Maestro? Call to rub in all the awesome sex you're having with your supermodel girlfriend?" He laughed again.

I chortled. "Not exactly."

"Uh oh. Trouble in paradise, eh?"

"Fuck, Dirk. You have no idea." I hesitated. "I don't even know why I'm calling you." I shrugged, not that he could see me, but I was overwrought, totally bent out of shape. "Guess you're the second-best thing to Tessa."

"Whoa… there's a bombshell." He yawned again. "So, fill me in. Did the day go the way you'd planned?"

"I mean, on paper, I guess so. We fucked, she worked, we went to the beach, played in the ocean, ate, fucked some more in the tub…"

He interrupted me, "Let me get this straight; the day didn't go the way you wanted it to? *Fuck me… no, fuck you*," he quipped sarcastically. "Life sure sounds rough." Before I could get a word in, he went on. "So, listen here, Garren. Stay focused. Pallavi was ripped away from you, through no fault of your own, and you were torn up about it. From the way you tell it, you searched years to find something even close to it again. Then, in walked Tessa. I get it. I do. But she's a Band-aid you stuck over the deep cut Vi left you with. Ditch the Band-aid and have the doctor who cut you sew you up whole."

I tried to get a word in, but he talked over me. "Seriously, Noah. Enough. Before Tessa, it was Vi this and Vi that. Now you're there, with Vi, and you're going to let the sassy red-head you met a few weeks ago mess this all up for you? Garren, dude! Wake the fuck up. You're blowing it!"

I sighed as I set my empty glass down on the table in front of me and motioned to Genevieve for a refill before resting my head in my hands. It hurt so fucking bad. "I don't know, Dirk," I struggled, "but Vi's different." I shook my head, "Maybe it's me who's different; in either case, *this* isn't working."

"Maybe you're not giving it a chance? I mean, have you asked yourself why you want Tessa now… over a fucking gorgeous supermodel, who's fallen head over heels for you? And that's just the icing—Suri's the cake. Have you even met her?"

"No." My voice wavered. "I love Tessa. It's just that simple. I mean; I tried, like you said, to put her out of my head…"

"It's been hours, Noah. How hard have you tried?"

"I don't give a fuck how long it's been, Dirk. I just know, okay?" I hadn't meant to get so angry, but what didn't he get? I didn't want Pallavi, I wanted Tessa.

"Sorry, man. Listen, I'm not trying to piss you off, but what if you come back here and Tessa's moved on? What if you've hurt her so badly that she's turned her heart off? Or, what if she does forgive you for putting her second and running off to be with Pallavi? You need to ask yourself if her forgiveness is genuine, and if deep-down she won't always feel that she's second-best to your first love. I mean, there's a lot you need to consider, brother, before you just up and throw Vi away like you're doing. I mean, what if you and she don't work out? I mean, will Tess even accept Suri? The memories that Suri brings with her could be too much for Tessa, you know?" I could picture him shrugging. Heard him light a cigarette and take a long drag off it.

"You're smoking?"

"Not really. Maybe. It just sounded good."

"Whatever. Just don't do that shit around me."

"No worries there. I've already butted it out." He chuckled. "Tasted like ass."

"Good man, good man." I rolled my neck and shook out my shoulders, trying to ease some of the tension. I took a long swig of the drink Genevieve had placed on the table before me. "Listen, I think my mind is pretty made up. I mean, I hear you, but my heart seems pretty settled on Tess."

"Noah, you called me for advice, right? So here it is—take notes," he kidded. "Don't think of Tess as a viable option, think of her as an addiction—a drug you need to get out of your system. If you think of her like that, then after you've gone through withdrawals, things will make more sense. I mean, you've only been there less than twenty-four hours."

What he was saying made *some* sense. I could at least give him that much. "Maybe you're right. I just wish she was here, so I could hear her voice. I've never wanted to talk to someone so badly. I pretty much feel the same way I did all those years ago, the morning after her going away party, now that I think of it. She shipped off, and I didn't have a name or number. All I wanted was to find out if she was the amazing angel that I'd thought she was the night before."

"See? She gets into your head, Garren. She messes with ya. Just give it some time. Vi will start looking more and more like the right choice, you'll see."

"Fuck, Dirk, you'd better sure as hell hope so... for your sake," I kidded.

We said our goodbyes and I hung up, tossing the phone on the table beside me. I slammed back the rest of my Jack and trudged off toward the suite.

-SEVEN-

I rolled over, away from the intrusive, painfully bright morning sun that shone through the opened wall of windows and reached out, but the sheets beside me were cold. *What the fuck?* Rolling over onto my back, I pulled myself against the headboard, dragging the sheet to my waist as I sat up. I looked around until I saw Pallavi sitting on the chaise lounge in only her tiny bikini bottoms, sunning herself in the early rays.

Sliding out of bed naked, I walked out onto the deck. I threw a folded towel onto the lounge beside her and lay back against the reclined chaise, immodest and unashamed; besides, my morning 'semi was nothing to blink at.

"Really, Noah?" She commented sardonically after her eyes took a sweeping appraisal of my body, lingering on my dick. I watched as she subconsciously ran her tongue across her lip, and now chewed on it.

"Like what you see?"

"Does it matter after the way you high-tailed it out of here last night?" She settled back into her seat and closed her eyes again, resting her shades over them.

"Yeah, well about that," I muttered. "Sorry. I was an insensitive ass."

"Mmm hmm."

"I just have a lot to sort through, ya know?" I closed my eyes, pensive and angry at myself. After my conversation with Dirk, I'd spent a good deal of time thinking. He'd had some solid points I hadn't considered, but mostly, I seemed to have a case of the 'grass is greener,' always thinking the other side of the fence looked better than the one I was on. Having given it some thought, I was ready to refocus and put more energy into making Pallavi and me work.

"Well, you'd better sort through them pretty darn quick, cause the nanny's supposed to be meeting us at the beach soon as we dock.

I breathed a sigh of relief. I was beginning to even wonder if she'd brought Suri with her. "Great. How long do I have?"

"What time is it?"

"11:20."

"Well, the manifest says we're supposed to anchor around noon," she stood up from her lounge and moved to my lap, straddling me, "which gives us *plenty* of time for me to take advantage of you before then." She reached down with both hands and stood my cock up, working it with her one hand, as she pulled the tiny strip of fabric between her legs aside.

"*Fuck me*," I hissed, as she slid me deeply into her velvet-soft pussy.

Pallavi's pace was not easy. She wanted me, and wanted me to know that she had no problem taking what she wanted. She bounced and gyrated on my heavy cock, working me closer to release.

She threw her head back, whimpering at the feel of my hard cock seated so deeply inside her. She was a goddess, her back arched, her hands behind her on my thighs for support, her neck elongated and her heavy breasts bouncing as she bucked and jerked on my straining rod.

I couldn't take much more. I knew my release was imminent, so I gripped her hip bones, ready to punish her pussy, hitting her G-spot repeatedly, until I could get her release. Measuredly, I slowed her assault, lifting her fully to the tip of my dick, then cramming her full. Slow and steady, inch by gritty inch, I targeted the bundle of nerves, stoking it repeatedly until she was quivering, begging for her release.

Vexed

"Please, Noah… please. I can't… I just, I can't…" she mewled and groaned.

"This, Vi. Remember this," I growled harshly, my restraint weakening. "This is why we work," I gritted out, "the best reason." And with that, I plowed deeply into her, firmly, roughly. My assault was intense and total. She cried out as she shattered, shuddered and trembled around my exploding cock. Her rippling orgasm milked mine to completion.

I strained for breath, wanting a cool shower before meeting my daughter. I lifted her wilted, waif-like frame off my lap and stood. I caught the back of the lounge for balance.

"Pretty fucking amazing, wasn't it?" she cooed, still too spent to move.

"Yeah, sure," I quipped, not in the mood to rehash the act. As good as it was, and as much as I talked myself into staying centered and focused on Vi, Tessa wasn't more than a breath away. I'd struggled badly enough all last night and this morning to keep her at bay, and now, I had to deal with the fucking guilt that I'd somehow cheated on her too.

Finding my balance, I strode into the master suite, grabbed my shorts and clean t-shirt from my pack and headed into the bathroom.

"Are you ready?" Pallavi stood at my side, arm around my waist, hugging me to her tightly. I couldn't put my finger on it, but she'd been unusually quiet after I'd gotten out of the shower. She seemed upset or maybe uneasy; hell, I had no idea how to interpret it, having been away from her all these past years, but she was *off.* Of that, I was sure. Best as I could figure, maybe she was pissed about how cavalier I'd been after our morning fuck on the deck.

We looked on over the top-deck railing as our yacht docked. I grabbed my backpack and threw it over my shoulder. I reached behind my back and, unhooking her arm from around my waist, took Pallavi's right hand in my left. "You okay?"

She nodded, looking edgy. I squeezed her hand and stopped her, willing her to look me in the eyes. Finally, her beautiful Persian eyes met my own.

"Okay… if you say so, but it seems like it should be me who's nervous. After all, I'm the one who has to win Suri over. What if she doesn't like me…?" My voice trailed off. "Should she call me Bâbâ, Papa, Dad, Daddy, Noah?"

"Relax. I'm sure whatever she calls you will come organically, and you'll be fine with any of them. You will, won't you?"

I smiled at her and squeezed her hand reassuringly as I started to walk us toward the stairs to the lower deck we'd disembark from.

The first step off the boat nearly launched me. As precise as the highly technical leveling system was on the yacht—and truth be told, I'd never felt the boat rock even an inch—my brain sure knew the fucking difference the instant my feet hit the wooden dock.

"I'd ask if you had your sea legs," she giggled, the first relaxed sign I'd seen from her today, "but," she continued, "what would you call this? Land legs?"

Her giggles were sweet and sexy, and I found myself chuckling in response. *Maybe today won't be as hard as I think it will be.*

Vexed

She took a sweeping glance at the dock, and, not seeing who she expected to be there, led me to a taxi that waited at the end by the storefronts. I opened the door for her and watched as she pulled her long, sexy, tan legs into the cab, before I slammed her door shut. I made my way around the back of the cab, taking one last look at the yacht. Then, the thought slammed into me. Either I'd make it work with Pallavi, and I'd see many more nights on a yacht like this one, or... this was potentially the last time I'd see a yacht like this, let alone spend the night on one acting as though I were the captain. *Well, it has been fun...*

What the fuck? Just like that, and that easily, I was talking to myself as though I were done with the yachting lifestyle, and inevitably, life with Pallavi. Not what I needed on my mind as I headed to see Suri.

"How'd you find this place," I asked as we pulled up the steep driveway to the Grande Bay Resort. "It seems a little off the beaten path. Besides, I'd have taken you for a private villa kind of girl." I gave her one of my drop-your-panties smiles.

"I wish," she said as the taxi slowed down, creeping to find her villa among the rows of resort villas. "This is about as luxurious as it gets here on the island, short of renting a privately-owned vacation home." She leaned forward to pay the cabbie. "Besides, our stay will be short. The plan is to leave tomorrow. We're taking the shoot to St. Thomas. Apparently,

Omar's assistant was sent out to recon a better beach and found it on the island next door."

We stepped out of the cab. I held Pallavi's elbow to steady her. She had worn ridiculous stilettos with her beach attire, and I'd bet only she could pull it off; on anyone else, it would look pretentious.

She walked slowly up to villa 1D. She rapped softly on the door, and someone I presumed to be either her nanny, Leah, or her assistant Rue opened it cautiously.

"Fuck! My pack!" I turned back towards the cab as he pulled away. "Wait up, hey! Just a second, you have my backpack!" I shouted loudly as I jogged out to the car and retrieved it from the backseat floorboards. I thanked the driver and closed the door.

-EIGHT-

Standing at the door, Pallavi was talking intimately with the gal who'd opened it. She was stroking the hair off the forehead of the young boy who sat on that woman's hip as the child clung to her. *Her nanny brought her kid? Kinda weird, but I guess it makes some sense… at least Suri always has someone to play with.*

I walked up to Pallavi and planted a kiss on her crown, inhaling deeply. She'd always smelled of rose water, even in Kuwait, something I'd never forget. I smiled at the woman and her kid. He was an attractive boy of maybe two or two and a half years, with dark skin and curly dark hair. He was tenfold better looking than she was, and I'd go so far as to say that he'd give Pallavi a run for her money once he got older. I tried to peek around the two of them, hoping to catch a glimpse of Suri.

Pallavi squeezed my hand and continued to hold on to it for dear life. She looked up at me timidly and back to the woman and her kid. "Noah, meet Saeed… *my son.*"

My breath caught in my chest. The muscles constricted, making it hard to breathe. I looked at her and back to him. "Hey, buddy," I said softly. Saeed's eyes tracked my movement as I reached out to gently touch his back. "Nice to meet ya. I'm Noah." I smiled, but the kid turned his face into the woman's neck and squirmed as though trying to climb her to get away from me. I looked questioningly at Pallavi, then the woman. "Nice to meet you…"

"Leah," she finished.

"Leah. You must be the nanny Vi's talked so much about," I continued hurriedly, not giving her a chance to either confirm or deny my assumption, "It's an honor to meet the other woman who's been raising my daughter in my absence." I smiled and looked down at Pallavi, squeezing her hand.

"Well, come on in," she said, stepping aside. "There's no point in us all standing outside in this heat."

Pallavi pulled me with her through the door and past Leah with Saeed. "I need a drink. Want one?" She dropped my hand and headed—with a clear mission in mind—toward the bar.

My eyes swept the room, looking for Suri… *fuck,* for any kind of evidence that a little girl was staying here. Sure, there were plenty of toys, but no dolls, no stuffed animals, not even a single pink item. *Where is she?* My thoughts became panicked. I looked toward the sliding glass door and balcony. *Did she fall?* I started to walk in that direction…

"Bourbon ok?" the question came from across the large room, stopping me in my tracks. "You take it with two cubes rig…"

"Cut the bullshit," I interrupted angrily. "Where's Suri?" I gesticulated toward the room with a large sweep of my hand. "Where's all of her toys? Is she okay?" I motioned toward the glass door and balcony that lay past it.

At this moment, Leah and Saeed were joining us in the great room. She stalled in her tracks, looking at Pallavi, then me, then back to her innocent charge's mother.

"Leah, leave us please."

Pallavi's face held a pleasant smile affixed to it, but her tone was nowhere even close to warm. In fact, it was fucking icy as hell. I watched as Leah grabbed the diaper bag and hurried down the hall. Seconds later, the door slammed closed.

Silence enveloped the room. A heavy, menacing silence that forbade me from moving any closer to Pallavi. I ran my hands across my face, scrubbing at it, trying to remove the anger already etched there. *If only Tess were here… I need you, baby.*

"Well," Pallavi's high pitched, nervous voice startled me from my thoughts of Tessa.

"Well, what?" I barked angrily. My pulse quickened as my breaths came more quickly. "Where the *fuck* is Suri?"

"It's complicated…"

Again, I interrupted her. "Jeezus, Vi, you'd better produce Suri… or so help me…"

"Or so help you what?" she barked as she threw the tongs back into the bucket of ice. "What'll you do to me that *HE* hasn't already?"

I eyed her dangerously, assessing her, trying to figure out what the hell was going on. I willed my pulse to slow and took deep, measured breaths. "You have two minutes to tell me what is going on, where Suri is, or you won't see me again. EVER." My eyes narrowed, willing her to test me.

"Can we please, *please*, just talk, Noah?"

"Answers, Vi. I need answers. You contacted me in Iceland and told me that it was over between you and your husband for good, that it had been for a long time, but you'd finally gotten the courage to leave. You told me you wanted me to come so I could meet my daughter." I took a deep breath, trying my best to stay calm and not be reactive. "Vi, Suri is why I'm here. You and me… we're only at our best when we fuck. With Suri, my emotions run deep. They're real. I've never met her, but I love her…" *Fuck*! I swore quietly under my breath, "Where is she?" My voice finally broke. "Why won't you let me meet her for Christ's sake?"

I moved robotically to a high-back leather chair and sat down heavily, resting my head in my hands. I couldn't rein in the overwhelming feeling that she was going to drop a life-changing bomb on me. Fear resounded in my soul and echoed through my thoughts.

I heard Pallavi making us drinks, and I looked up as she walked over to me, placing a whiskey glass in my hand. She took a seat on the ottoman directly in front of me, and I watched distractedly as she removed her stilettos with her free hand. She crossed her tan legs and rested her arms on them.

How can she be this composed? What the fuck is going on? I could feel my muscles tightening, my teeth clenching and my pulse quickening. My eyes once again swept the room, hoping, *praying*, that I'd see Suri standing innocently in the doorway, wiping the sleepys from her eyes, holding an armful of dollies. *At least that would explain where all the fucking dolls are…*

"Noah," she sighed heavily, "Suri…" her voice trailed off and she shook her head violently enough that it sloshed the cubes in her glass, their clanking loud against the silence in the room. "Suri Noa-Garren Amrav was never born," she choked out unevenly.

A gut-wrenching pain hit me at my core, then crept up, threatening to consume me. "Wait, *wait*…" I muttered in disbelief and confusion. "I… I, don't understand. You, we… lost her? Our baby girl?" Tears pricked my eyes, and I felt like I couldn't breathe.

"No, Noah." Her tone changing from nervous to suddenly dismissive and unfeeling. "What don't you get? She was never real—I just said that to get you back."

I sat in stunned silence, my brain frenetically working to make sense of what I'd just heard. *Suri was never real? My baby girl? Fucking BITCH!* My mind swirled, angry, hurt, and in complete and total disbelief. Shock. I didn't want to hear anything else the lying cunt had to say. I willed my legs to move, but they ignored me, so I sat there paralyzed.

"I figured," she went on in a grossly inappropriate sing-song voice, "that if you thought we had a little girl, you'd come back to me. I was done with Ahmed… you know that," she hurriedly prattled. "He beat me. I left my motherland, my family, all of it to be with you." She set her glass down beside the ottoman and reached out for my hands, which rested on my knees, weakly holding onto my whiskey glass.

"You lied." My voice was steel, cold and unwavering. I felt my emotions tighten as they sealed back inside my heart. "You lied, Vi. About our child, no less. How could you?" I shook my head in disgust.

She reached out for me a second time, her fingertips burning my skin where they made contact.

"DON'T fucking touch me." I looked up into her exotic eyes with my own hardened gaze. "All you do is hurt me, Vi. Ahmed came back, and you didn't even offer me so much as a goodbye. Nine months later, you call me to tell me I have a daughter but offered no other info, which hurt me—devastated me actually—but what was I going to do? You chose him, so I kept away, so as not to ruin your home life. Damn it, Vi!" Emotion exploded out of me. I was so angry that I fucked everything up with Tessa because I had to see what life would have been like with Pallavi. *Well, now you know, dumbass. It's all been a fucking lie. All of it.*

I stood up and pushed past her, throwing back the cold three-ounce pour she'd brought me. I walked to the bar counter, savoring the last of the aged bourbon as it slid with consolatory ease down my constricted throat. I didn't want to look at her, for fear her wiles would ease the all-consuming hatred I now felt for her. I didn't want to forgive her. I wanted her to understand what she'd done to me.

"Six years, Vi. Six years passed before you called me. Damn it, the night before you called me, I met again the *one* woman who might have truly let me be me. Who," I searched for the right words… *if only Pallavi can understand the ruin she's caused*, "who loves me as deeply as I now know I love her." I reached up and swiped at the tears dampening my eyelashes. *God, I miss Tess. I love her so much, and she may never know.* That thought—along with the painful realization that all the thoughts of a future being Suri's dad were for nothing—overtook me. *Bitch!*

I turned around, and upon seeing her looking angelic and completely nonchalant, a vile disgust for Pallavi flooded my mouth and invaded my spirit. "Vi," I seethed, "I have never, EVER, felt hatred toward anyone before... but I HATE you, you and your bullshit manipulations. I hate everything you are. You are poison to my heart, mind and soul, and I never, and I mean *NEVER* want to see or hear from you again." I held my composure as the rage built inside me. All I wanted to do now was get home so that I could see my baby... Tessa. That is, if she'd have me back.

I walked past Pallavi where she stood, her mouth agape as she stared at me. When I reached the door, she rushed me, trying to close the distance between us, arms open as though I'd even consider giving her a goodbye hug. I flung the door open, and before pulling it behind me, I stared her down until she stopped in her tracks.

"I nearly forgot one thing," I spat. "FUCK YOU!" As it rolled off my lips, my sneer transformed into a genuine smile as the weight of Pallavi and her drama rolled off my shoulders for good.

Vexed

-NINE-

I shifted uncomfortably on the phone booth stool and looked down the long row of public cubicles that lined the wall in the busy concourse I'd been passing the hours in. After Pallavi revealed the depth of her deception, I'd hightailed it out of there back to St. Thomas as quick as I could, and from there, found myself waiting out the remaining two hours of my eight-hour layover in San Juan, Puerto Rico at the Luis Muñoz Marín International Airport.

"Hello?"

"Hi, Mom."

"Noah! Oh my gosh, David! Noah's on the phone!"

I smiled at her excitement but felt uncomfortable and shocked at hearing her call for my dad. My dad, who hadn't lived with her since their divorce years ago. "Dad's there? Are you okay?" My brow furrowed, and I scrubbed my hands over my face, trying to alleviate my concern. "Mom! Are you okay?"

"Shh, shh, Noah. I'm fine."

"Is Dad okay? Why's he there? Did you guys get back… *together*?"

"David, Noah wants to know why you're here. Do you want to tell him or should I?"

"Mom! Out with it already. What's going on?"

"You know Noah, he's getting himself all worked into a tizzy…"

"Mom!" I could hear her handing off the phone off and talking, but I couldn't make out what she was saying. I shook my head and could only imagine what I looked like, all red-faced and irritated.

"Nohwie?"

I froze. My mind swirled trying to place the mature female voice who was using the nickname that only *she* had ever used. It made no sense. *Who …? What, I mean… how? I mean, it makes no sense. She's been gone since I was twelve. Kidnapped. How is this possible?* I couldn't bear to hear myself call this *other* woman by *her* name.

"Nohwie? It's me… your sister, Lisa." she paused, but there was only silence on my end.

"Noah?" My father's harsh voice replaced the soft, not quite frail, but delicate female one. "For Christ's sake, say something. We have you on speaker."

"Dad?" I muttered, my voice foreign to even my ears. "What the hell's going on here?" I took a moment to draw in a deep, labored breath… steadying my nerves. "Jeezus fuck, Dad… Will someone please explain to me what the fuck's going on? This *isn't* funny… AT ALL." I looked around, suddenly aware of how loud I was being, to see if anyone had taken notice. *Thank God no one seems to give a shit…*

"Son, we've been waiting to tell you when the time was right, after we were sure…"

I interrupted, "Sure? You waited until you were sure? All this time you've said nothing?" I croaked. "Lisa's back?" Upon saying her name, my voice broke, and years of fear and pent-up emotion surrounding her disappearance and my parents' separation flooded my usual, put-together demeanor.

"When you didn't come to find me, I got worried, Noah. I was so scared, somehow I wandered farther than I ever had in the woods behind our house."

My mother interrupted. "Lisa got mixed up; she was so young."

"Yes. I ended up wandering onto someone's property. I was crying, and a woman came out of her small cabin and she and her husband said they called the police to report me, but were told that our home had caught on fire."

I wept silently, watching person after person rush past with their carry-ons, scurrying through the busy airport terminal like ants along a trail. *Why did she believe we all died? Did they even call the police to report her? Where did they go and why didn't she ever try to find out more about us?*

My mind refocused on what my dad was saying. "From what Lisa told us, they immediately moved—he said it was for business…"

"Yes," Lisa added. "We moved to New York for a short time—actually flew out the next morning—and then moved to London shortly after. I was so young, and they were so nice I just believed them that the police had asked them to care for me, since I had no one."

What about as you got older? Didn't you have any questions about who these people were? Why you moved so far away? Didn't you ever research the fire? There were so many questions I wanted to ask, but I failed as my mind struggled with my changing reality. The new paradigm shifted years of clear history aside, as a new, muddled and hazy one surfaced. *How is this possible? My sister Lisa is alive? My little sister is back in my life? If only I had Tessa around to share this with…*

"I couldn't help overhearing…"

I cracked my eyes and looked toward the direction of the coarse voice that had just interrupted my meditative, pre-slumber state.

"You overheard what, man?" I sat up, kicking my pack under the narrow airplane seat in front of me. Someone jostled my shoulder as they pushed past looking for their row.

"Flying coach fucking sucks," I groused under my breath. I sighed and took a better look at the male sitting next to the window. The empty seat between us gave us a nice buffer. He was a sturdy-looking individual: crew-cut, clean-shaven, and I noticed a military squadron ball cap attached to the backpack at his feet. "Military?" I inquired without much interest.

"Yup. Navy."

I nodded. "Heading back from leave or taking it?"

He smiled pleasantly and nodded down to the papers resting atop his lap. "Hell, I only wish. I'm headed off to Iceland on a new set of orders." He shifted and extended his hand toward me, "Edward Beye. Nice to meet a fellow brother." He raised his eyebrow, questioning if he'd called it right by assuming I was military too. Considering we were flying commercial and not military charter, it was a risky assumption.

"Marines. Ren. Nice to meet you too," I offered as I took his hand and shook it. "Iceland, huh? So, you're ready for this?" I chuckled.

He looked at me skeptically, eyeing me to determine if I was giving him shit or speaking from experience. "What do you know of it?" he finally spat defensively, then looked past me to the other passengers who were still filing in to take their seat assignments.

I cleared my throat. "I'm on a security billet at NAS Keflavik. You'll do fine so long as you realize it isn't a base like stateside, and you won't be attached to a squadron per se…"

He looked back at me directly. "Yeah, once I arrive I'll be attached to OMD, the Organizational Maintenance Department."

Again, I nodded. "NATO support, eh? Well, that's a good place to be attached to. They'll keep you busy for sure. A busy schedule helps pass the time, and it'll keep ya out of trouble." I chuckled and smiled encouragingly, "So, you're a mechanic?"

"Nah, there's no way I could be a grease monkey. I'm a wire chaser, an aviation electrician."

"Really?" I mused. "I just ended a relationship with an AE."

Edward laughed good-naturedly. "Isn't that how it goes… on again, off again… mostly off for me. I've been divorced for a while now, so I totally hear ya. Maybe sometime we could meet up for a beer and a game of pool? You could introduce me to the Icelandic scene?" He looked at me hopefully, and I acquiesced, knowing how hard it was to arrive on a new base, at a new squadron and be totally alone.

"Well, I'm sure we'll run into each other at the base pub, The Privateer." I pulled out my CD player, slapped in one of my favorite Dave Matthews CDs, and plugged the buds into my ears, denoting that I was done with this conversation. I looked over at… *What did he say his name was?—Edward something?*—and smiled at him, before I closed my eyes, settling in for the long, direct flight back to Iceland.

Tina Maurine

-TEN-

"Jeezus, man. I'm sure glad to see you." I closed the gap between Dirk and me and embraced him briefly in a brotherly hug.

"Well, shit… If I didn't know better, I'd say you missed me," he kidded. "Glad to be back?"

"Fuck, buddy. You have NO idea." Truly, he didn't—couldn't know the shit I'd been through these past few days. "I can't wait to get back to business as usual."

"Well, come on then. Got your bag, or we need to go get it?" He nodded toward the small, unimpressive luggage carousel alongside the waiting area where I'd met him.

"Nah, man, this is all I took." I held up my old backpack and thought back to the numerous times its worn canvas and scarred leather bottom had served me well over the years.

"See ya, Ren!"

I turned in to see the guy who'd sat beside me in the plane. "Sure thing, Beye." I waved. "Look for Dirk and me at the Privateer. We'll be hitting it up this weekend for sure."

"Sounds good. See ya then!" He waved a single time and stepped through the sliding doors into the harsh Icelandic winds.

"Who's he?" Dirk motioned toward the parking lot entrance.

"Just a newb. Took orders with OMD."

He nodded, and the two of us headed through the double doors and out into the brisk elements. I shivered. "Fuck, man!"

"Cold eh?" He laughed at my discomfort. "I didn't know heading to the Caribbean for such a short amount of time would turn you into a pussy."

I jokingly glared at him, "Shut the fuck up. I might be a pussy, but you're a pansy-ass motherfucker!" He elbowed me and we jested all the way to the duty van he'd brought to pick me up.

I pulled open the heavy truck door and slid onto the brown, worn pleather seat.

"So, man… what happened? Back with Vi?"

I grunted and slid down, resting my head on the back of the bench seat. "No."

"How did it go meeting Suri? I bet she's a beauty, from the photos I've seen of her mother."

"She was another of Vi's fucked up lies." I sighed heavily. "She never existed."

I heard him draw in a sharp intake of breath. He then slowly let out a whistle. "No shit? Wow, man. Sorry."

I closed my eyes as I scrubbed my hands over my face. *Yeah, tell me about it. I'm sorry too…*

Sorry the vision of fatherhood was ripped from me.

Sorry I'd put trust back in Pallavi's devious hands, only for her to toy with me.

Sorry I'd wasted precious leave and tons of money on a useless vacation.

But mostly, I was sorry I'd hurt Tessa.

God, I wish I hadn't ended things with her—ended good, sure, and concrete things with such an amazing woman who loved me for me—on a mere whim of a maybe. All of this messed up bullshit with Pallavi had helped me see what I'd given up. *Now all I can do is pray my Tessa will take me back…*

The End

Also by Tina Maurine

Look for: Volition
A Uniform & Lace Romance
Book One: Noah & Tessa's Story

Look for: Impasse
A Uniform & Lace Romance
A novella in the *For the Love of Politics Anthology* by: Wild Dreams Publishing

Look for: Rhodes to Desire
A novella in the *Hushed Affairs Anthology* by: Wild Dreams Publishing

Tina Maurine

Look for: Brother in Arms
A novelette in the *Just Love Anthology* by: Crazy Ink
Publishing

Look for: Destiny Scent
A novelette in *Kissing Midnight, A New Year's Eve Anthology*
by: Crazy Ink Publishing

Coming soon: Veneration
A Uniform & Lace Romance
Book Two: Noah & Tessa's Story
~An excerpt is at the back of this book~

Acknowledgments

First I want to thank God for instilling my love of writing and for giving me the gift of expression through writing. There were many times I wondered if I were on the right path, but I always came back to Him and when I did I became refocused and confident in my choices. Writing centers me and genuinely makes me happy.

To my family—my husband and kids—who never complain when my face is staring at a screen and my hands are making music on the keys. You're never angry that my spare time is spent writing stories and creating other worlds. Thanks for understanding and always supporting me.

To Lisa… for giving me the idea of this story-in-between… way back in 2015. Without our late-night 'til 3am brainstorming sessions, *Vexed* wouldn't have started taking shape. So, thanks, Hun!

To Jude… because in this writing world, you are my ROCK. You listen, and always lift me up when I'm just not sure I'm good enough. I love ya, chica!

To Kristi & Bec… for your support and no bullshit friendship. You are book-reading, book-pimping queens and I never even have to ask! You always have my back and offer feedback whenever I needed it. Without you, I'd never have made it as far as I have in this Indie world.

Tina Maurine

To Simone… for your friendship and prioritizing me amidst your way too-full schedule. Your editing polishes my stories, and this one was no exception. I value all of your input and thank you for your honesty. I cannot thank you enough.

Lastly, to the amazing crew at Wild Dreams Publishing: Melissa, YM, ML, Katie and all the other women who support me by pimping my books, THANK YOU! THANKS TO ALL the others who have read my books and reviewed them. Without your help, I'd never sell a book. So again, thank you!

Vexed

Excerpt from

Veneration

A Uniform & Lace Romance
Noah & Tessa's Story
~Book Two~

"Dirk's been telling me about Noah since he got back. I guess his trip was cut short, and then there's Ari. I mean it all just piled up—you having everyone and me feeling like I don't really have anyone. So, anyways… sorry for being all jealous and shit, and for lashing out at you." Her apology gushed from her like a breath held too long that explodes out, uncontainable and forceful. I gave her a comforting smile and another quick hug to reassure her that all was fine between us.

Noah's back? He got back early?!

I peeked around the corner of the doorjamb, and Lucas's eyes connected with mine. They grew large as he rolled them, and then, giving his head a little nod, he tried to tell me to get our asses back in there.

"First of all… everyone does not want me. Secondly, YOU have got to catch me up on Trigg and you—Ketts and Dane. Thirdly," as I took a deep breath, my chest involuntarily constricted, "you need to fill me in about Dirk and Noah." I had planned on having a *fourthly*—if there is such a thing—and even a finally, but after just saying Noah's name, I couldn't get anything else out.

"Let's go rescue the guys." Sammie threw a head nod in the direction of the kitchen. "I'll catch you up later."

As we walked in, the two Aviation Technicians (ATs) who worked with the guys in the intermediate-level shops back home stood up from their chairs, and smiled as they walked past us. Lucas rose, grabbing seconds and offering to get us more, but I was having a hard time getting through all the food he'd already served me before Sammie pulled me into the hallway.

Ace was the first to speak, after taking a long draw from his beer. "So, everything fine with you two? Is your lover's spat finally over?" He chuckled and I raised my beer to him, tipping it in a sarcastic toast.

"We're fine. It's just, this deployment can really get to ya sometimes, right, Sam?"

She nodded at me, smiling back.

"So, let me get this right. You guys worked for like three days on your detachment to Turkey—that's it, and you were gone a week?" Incredulity hung heavy in his tenor. "What did you guys do Friday, Saturday and Sunday?" Lucas had reseated himself at the table after grabbing us all a new, ice-cold brewski from the fridge.

"Well, the officers and aircrew still had to fly two more days with the NATO forces, so we readied the birds the first day, packed up a shit-load of parts we never used, tools and materials, so we'd be ready to jet out Monday—then we did some sightseeing." I paused to shovel another bite of calzone heaven into my mouth, washing it down with my beer, which seemed to get better and better with each swig I drew off it.

"Okay, so other than the coastline, which I'm assuming you liked, what was the best thing you saw while you were there?"

I turned my head, startled to hear a voice coming from behind me—a *very* familiar voice. My eyes connected instantly to deep pools of blue—stormy, grey-blue eyes that I had missed for too long, and yet not long enough to move on…

…if I ever could.

I sat paralyzed, glancing at everyone at the table and then turning to look back at Noah as he walked around to my side.

"Well, get up and come give me a hug!" His playful command came out in an emotionally laden tone, walking the line his voice took when it was full of lust and desire.

Oh. My.

I stood mechanically at first, and then I rushed him. My heart winning out over my mind, I threw my arms around his neck as he pulled me to him tightly for a full-body hug. Everything about me that felt skewed the last few days immediately righted themselves and our souls drew together like magnets, each recharged off of what the other offered. It was a truly carnal and nearly supernatural thing, how we connected so completely. So borderline indecently.

Noah's arms wrapped around my waist, pulling me into his already thickening desire for me. His arm shifted, crossing my back, pressing my taut nipples into his thin, t-shirt clad chest. His hand, nesting at the nape of my neck, guided my lips towards his. I could feel his breath coming in short, hot pants— mirroring my own. His lips grazed mine, eliciting a shudder from me. Then he kissed me, delicately at first, then more fully.

It was a kiss that didn't just tell me things, it screamed confirmations about how much he'd missed me… and then our lips began a lascivious dance—pulling, drinking, robbing the other's senses.

"Fuck, why don't you just kiss her already?" Ace quipped, and then laughed as I heard his beer bottle tap two others behind me in a toast.

I pulled my ravished lips from Noah's skillful ones, only able to drag in ragged breaths. My emerald eyes once again connected to his gaze—now a heated cerulean hue.

Goddamn, he's hot. I lov... I caught myself before I admitted the depth of my feelings for him. I just couldn't go there—Vi and Suri were still swimming around in the back of my mind. *What had happened on Saint John?*

He smiled a wicked little half smile at me before placing a chaste kiss on my forehead. He spun me around and, placing either hand on my hips, pulled my ass to him. I leaned back against him in a reverse full body hug—we didn't need our arms for our bodies to connect completely. I blushed, remembering the things he had done to me the last time he'd placed his hands on my hips like this…

"So, Tessa…" Lucas cleared his throat, obviously turned on to a degree by what he'd just seen, which was understandable, seeing as how he was remaining completely faithful to his wife back home and it had been a couple weeks shy of three months since we'd left Jacksonville. "…about what Noah asked. What did you like the best while you were there?"

I pushed my ass off the substantially hard cock I'd been resting against and playfully negotiated Noah off the fridge door. "Anyone care for another beer?" I ended up pulling out a total of five, opened them and passed them around. I took a seat at the table, and Noah pulled up a chair beside me, taking my fork and shoveling a large bite from my calzone into his mouth.

"Well, one day we went to Incirlik and the other to Adana, both pretty close to the base. We actually went to Incirlik a few times with a handful of guys and gals stationed there and some guys from the Royal Airforce. The small village-town was within walking distance about twenty minutes away, and there were some local watering holes—dives really—that stayed open late, especially if we were there spending money."

"Yeah, I've been down Incirlik's narrow, dingy, dirt road more than a few times, coming and going from ops out of Kuwait, but Adana's markets are a whole lot more fun to get lost in, especially if you're drinking, wouldn't you agree?" Noah laughed, knowing full well that I knew better than to get trashed and then try to sightsee and keep my bearings. I was way too much about being in control to let myself let lose in that kind of a situation.

Any situation really… unless Tad was the one taking away my control.

The slightest blush crept up my cheeks to my ears. I prayed no one noticed, so I quickly went on. "Yeah, I mean hanging with the crew at night was fun, and I bought a great black leather cigar jacket from Incirlik, but you're right; if I'd had more time I would've definitely gone back to Adana… after all, it was only like five or ten miles away, and *oh man,* the shopping I could've done!" I giggled and Sammie snorted. She knew I was a total shopaholic.

"Get anything good in Adana? Buy anything extra that I could buy from you and send to my wife?"

"Oh, Lucas, I'm sorry, but the best thing I picked up was a pair of leather string sandals… the soles are made from tires. Oh, and I picked up a pretty marble backgammon board for my dad, and an ornate scarf for Tulla Dean." I watched Lucas's eager, hopeful eyes turn dismal. "Oh wait, I have some Turkish Delight that you can send her!"

Lucas looked at me cautiously, "What the *fuck* is a Turkish Delight—some kind of sex toy?"

Oh, my Gawd!! Now that's too funny...

"No, stupid," I said good-naturedly, as I laughed. "Turkish Delight is a gummy, marshmallowy treat made of dried nuts, fruits, syrup, and some other shit. It's a national favorite. I personally hate the stuff, but to each his own. I bought a bunch 'cause everyone was raving about how great it was—and Kupps bargained for it and got it for a really good price. It's known as lokum in Turkish—a word also used to refer to a voluptuous woman." I giggled, "Now *that* I learned having a shot of elixir in some rug shop; Kupps actually knew where the closest pastane or souvenir shop was from there." My soliloquy died on my lips and I quickly brought the beer to my lips and took a long hard draw, giving me plenty of time to take a breath and think...

Oh shit. Kupps...

Did Noah pick up on that or anyone else? FUCK! How many beers have I had? Four, maybe? Damn, I should've eaten more...

I looked over at Sammie, and she raised an eyebrow at me, then at Lucas. He looked at me and cleared his throat.

"Oh, okay so Kupps is from your shop? You work with him?" Noah's tenor hitched a bit at the end, obviously nervous about how I'd answer his questions.

"Yeah, pretty much."

Okay, so Kupps *was* basically from my shop... I mean *so what* if he was the Division Officer? Nobody sitting at the table could really go about hearing what I had to say and then throw stones. Noah didn't *REALLY* need to know all the specifics. Besides, he did just get back from seeing his baby's mama, and I am *SURE* they fucked up one side and down the other… that is, after all, what Noah does well.

I hurriedly went on so that he wouldn't continue along that line of questioning. "So, I have a few bars that you're more than welcome to; in fact, there are probably enough for all of you to have some."

I didn't have to glance at Noah to feel his heated gaze on me. He gave me a rough squeeze on my thigh. I jumped just a little, and a nervous giggle escaped. "So, what did you guys do while I was gone for the week?" I eyed the table, and then looked squarely at Noah. "How was *your* visit with Pallavi and Suri?"

Noah stood up, lifting me by my elbow. "Join me in the hall, Tessa?" His steely tone left no room for argument. As he briskly led me toward the door I tossed out a flippant, "I'll be right back, guys—don't do anything I wouldn't do!"

I heard someone shout, "That's doesn't really limit us very much!" and they all laughed.

Tina Maurine

About the Author

Tina Maurine is the gal on the sidelines at the party. The gal who smiles at everyone, but rarely initiates conversation; never the center of attention, but always taking notes on those who are. She loves watching people, their authentic responses to everyday occurrences and in turn has turned years of notes into fodder for her stories, an encyclopedia of emotions and character traits that come alive on the page. She never feels more alive than when she is creating; be it stories, music, graphic art, or painting rocks and canvases with her daughter.

Tina Maurine

She is a wife, mom, best friend, secretary, teacher, cheerleader, house-straightener, chef, chauffeur, video game playing, Barbie doll dressing domestic multi-tasker. She likes her French baguettes crispy, her beer dark, and her chocolate even darker. Her music tastes are eclectic, but if there's a beat, you can bet her body is moving to it… even in the car… and the louder the better.

Tina Maurine lives in Oregon with her amazing husband of twelve years, and their two beautiful children. Prior to marriage and children, she served eight years in the United States Navy and saw the world. She and her husband share their love for travel with their kids, and take as many family trips as their busy schedules allow. When they aren't hitting the road or the skies, and when she isn't teaching, Tina is content to sit at the table in their backyard with her keyboard or a good, sexy book, and watch the kiddos play.

Follow her on Twitter and Instagram @ TinaMaurineAuth
Email: tinamaurine@hotmail.com
http://facebook.com/tina.maurine.1
http://tinamaurine.com